Choke

by

Kaye George

Mainly Murder Press, LLC
PO Box 290586
Wethersfield, CT 06129-0586
www.mainlymurderpress.com

Mainly Murder Press

Copy Editor: Jennafer Sprankle
Executive Editor: Judith K. Ivie
Cover Designer: Karen A. Phillips

Mainly Murder Press
www.mainlymurderpress.com

Copyright © 2011 by Kaye George
ISBN 978-0-9827952-7-9

Published in the United States of America

2011

Mainly Murder Press
PO Box 290586
Wethersfield, CT 06109-0586

Dedication

~ For Mom ~

Acknowledgments

I've been helped in my writing career by more people than I can name here, but I can mention a few, at least. Thanks so much to Avery Aames, Krista Davis, Sharon Oliver, Susan Schreyer, and Pat Brown who all read early versions of this title. The Austin Mystery Writers have been shaping my writing for years: Karen McInerney, Mary Jo Powell, Kimberley Sandman, Mark Bentsen, and more recently, Kathy Waller and Gale Albright.

My wonderful Guppy critique group, James Montgomery Jackson, Cathy Sonnenberg, Kristy Blank Makansi, and Cher'ley Grogg gave me loads and loads of helpful input. Classes I've taken from Mary Buckham, Kris Neri, Margie Lawson, and Pat Kay improved my writing abilities, and I wholeheartedly recommend their classes. The encouragement I've gotten from Nan Higginson and Janet Reid, and the help from Melissa Collier, Joel at Pak Mail, have kept me going. I know I've left some out, but thank you all.

—

One

"That's it, Uncle Huey!" Imogene Duckworthy whipped off her apron and flung it onto the slick, stainless steel counter. "I quit!" If only her voice didn't sound so young. Her order pad, pencil, even the straws skittered out of their pouches and across the floor. She took a step back, her shoes sticking to the trod-upon-after-lunch debris of squished lettuce, blobs of gravy, and bits of unidentifiable brown stuff.

"You can't quit, darlin'," drawled Uncle Huey in that thin, nasal voice that made him seem six inches shorter than his five-ten. "You're family." He dipped a scoop of mashed potatoes onto a plate, ladled thick brown gravy on top, and handed it to the cook.

"I'm not working double shifts again next week." Immy hoped she sounded serious. Mature. Convincing.

"Well, you'll just have to, won't you? Since Xenia just quit on me today, you and April are all the waitresses I've got left."

Clem, the portly cook, piled the hot plate with thick slabs of meatloaf, spooned green beans beside them, and shoved it into April's waiting hands. Immy hadn't eaten lunch yet, and the oniony smell of the meatloaf kicked up some saliva under her tongue. She watched April swing through the double doors and glimpsed the whitewashed dining room full of scarred wooden tables and chairs, almost empty of customers now.

She'd worked and played in this restaurant her entire twenty-two years. It had been started by her grandparents and handed down to her father and her uncle. Since her father's death, of course, Uncle Huey had run it alone.

Would she miss this place? Maybe, but she was quitting anyway.

Immy pounded her fist on the work counter. Hugh Duckworthy jumped. "No, Uncle Huey. April is all you've got left, and if you'd kept your mitts to yourself, you'd still have Xenia." Immy's hands shook as she snatched her purse and jacket from her cubby, but she succeeded in stomping out the back door of the diner, past the cook and busboy who were staring open-mouthed. Aside from troublesome customers, she didn't talk back to people often, even when she wanted to.

Uncle Huey may have been her father's brother, but he was a first class jerk.

In the alley she paused beside the dumpster. Leaned against the sun-warmed metal. Gulped a big breath of relief. And choked on the stench of rotting vegetables. She moved a little farther from the dumpster for her next breath and collapsed against the brick wall, trembling in the aftermath of her bravery.

Immy closed her eyes and let the Texas sun soak into her upturned face, willing it to calm her. She turned her mind to the future. A purchase was waiting for her in Wymee Falls, but she had no transportation to pick it up. What should she do now? She tried to focus.

"What in the hell got into you, Immy?"

Her eyes flew open at the sound of the deep voice. Baxter, one of Huey's two busboys, emptied a bin of food scraps into the dumpster, plunked it onto the alley paving, and strolled over to stand a couple of feet from her. Her pulse raced at the closeness of his lean, hard body. Damn, that man was handsome.

Immy had had a crush on Baxter Killroy since he started to work in the diner two and a half years ago, even though he was at least ten years older than Immy, mid-thirties.

"I never heard you talk back to the boss like that before."

That lazy smile drew her closer. She pushed off the brick wall and took a step toward him. Her mind always messed up in front of a handsome man. "Well, I guess I never did before."

"Gotta admire that in a woman. That's spunk, Immy."

She glowed at his approval, feeling her face flush. She didn't think Baxter had ever thought of her as a woman before. To avoid falling into those deep, dark eyes, she looked over Baxter's shoulder. On the other side of the dumpster stood two pickups, Huey's and Baxter's. An idea formed.

"Say, I have a little problem," she said. "You don't suppose I could borrow your pickup to go into Wymee Falls, do you?"

He shrugged. "Don't see why not. I'm tied up here until the end of my shift, since I'm not quitting today. It needs gas. Can you bring it back full and have it here by closing?" He reached into his back jeans pocket and tossed her the keys.

Immy surprised herself by catching them.

"Hey," said Baxter. "You catch pretty good for such a scrawny gal."

She wasn't certain scrawny was a compliment, but being a good catch was. She'd take what she could get from him. She climbed into the pickup and backed into the alley, giving Baxter a wave. As she drove out of Saltlick, she couldn't help clenching a fist, yelling, "Yee haw," and pounding Baxter's grimy steering wheel. She was free. She had quit. Little, mousy Immy had shown gumption. Yes, she had. Even Baxter admired her for it. And she had an important, secret errand to run. The world was wide open to her without that job tying her down.

During the noon rush, Immy had watched in jaw-dropping awe as Xenia whirled on Uncle Huey, who had just pinched her bottom for the ten thousandth time, smacked his hand, as usual, then walked out, which had never happened before.

Soon after, when most of the lunch crowd was gone, something had reared up inside Immy, something she could no longer deny. It wasn't that she minded hard work. She could sling hash and run her legs off with the best of them, but that wasn't what she wanted to do with her life. It didn't coincide with her burning desire, her goal.

She had talked herself into thinking she hated working in the diner, hated working for Uncle Huey, hated waiting tables, period. There was a big, wide world outside Saltlick, Texas, population one thousand, two hundred, thirty-four, and it was waiting for Imogene Duckworthy. First step, pick up the purchase that would be a stepping stone.

It shouldn't be a problem getting another job to tide her over until she could land her dream position. The Wymee Falls paper was full of want ads every day, wasn't it? True, she hadn't looked lately, but it used to be.

She drove toward Wymee Falls, the nearest sizeable town and the county seat, to pick up the order she had placed over a week ago. On her way, driving past barbed-wire-fenced stretches of flat, sparse grassland dotted with distant cattle herds, she rehearsed what she would tell her mother. She rejected one scenario after another.

Immy drove past the fake, man-made waterfall at the edge of town. Her life lately reminded her of that waterfall, pointlessly going up and down, in and out, over and over, never making progress. It was time for her to do something for herself. Days, weeks, months were fleeting past, leaving her in the dust with a minimum wage job while her dream floated out of reach, seeming to recede more and more rapidly into the distance. She was going after that dream before it disappeared.

IMMY CROSSED HER SPARSELY GRASSED West Texas front yard. The lawn hadn't greened up so early in the season that passes for spring in these parts. She tiptoed up the steps to the single-wide and opened the door. After returning Baxter's truck to the diner, she had walked the short distance home.

"Imogene, dear? Is that you?"

Busted by those ancient, squeaky hinges.

"Yes, Mother," she shouted over the strains of a soap opera theme. Even though she didn't see Mother in her recliner, Immy was not going to make it to her bedroom undetected.

Her mother filled the doorway from the kitchen, a frown above her wobbling chins. "What are you doing home this time of day?"

Immy gritted her teeth and smiled. "Uncle Huey let me go early today, Mother." Her carefully rehearsed excuse sounded phony as she said it. She was such a lousy liar. Immy shrugged her sweater off and threw it onto the battered pine bench next to the door, attempting casual, ordinary movement. Did she look as stiff as she felt? She also didn't want to tell her mother where she'd been for the last hour. Mother would not approve of her purchase.

Her mother's look changed from almost worried to definitely worried. "What about your remuneration? Will he compensate you for the remainder of your shift?"

A small knot formed in Immy's stomach. "Um, sure. I'm sure he will. I'll go back, um, tomorrow and he'll …"

"What aren't you telling me, Imogene? You know I can always perceive your prevarications."

Big sigh. Yes, she always could. Might as well fess up. "I, well, I don't work there anymore." Immy cringed, anticipating the explosion.

"He fired you? He terminated his niece? His only living relative? That scumbag. Who does he think he is? He's gonna hear from me, I'll tell ya." Hortense stumped to the hall closet, shaking the whole trailer, and yanked her jacket off its hanger.

Immy had previously noticed that her mother's erudite vocabulary vanished under stress. It made her chuckle sometimes, but not now. Her stomach roiled around a hard, growing knot. She had never lied to her mother, except for a small fib or two, nothing like this.

"Mother, wait."

But Mrs. Hortense Duckworthy was out the door, stomping down the wooden steps.

"Dammit, listen to me," Immy yelled from the doorway. "He didn't terminate me, I quit." Whew. That felt good. Even at her advanced age of twenty-two, Immy wasn't accustomed to cussing at her mother. Cussing and lying in the same day. She was going to hell.

When Hortense reached the asphalt road at the edge of the yard, she stopped, hunched her shoulders, then turned and called back, "Why the hell did you quit? Where do y'all think money's gonna come from? The moon?"

"Mother, stop yelling. Come back here, and I'll tell you about it."

Immy returned to the worn living room and sagged into the soft couch. Her mother must have refilled the lemon-scented plug-in recently. Immy could tell because her nose started to drip. She kicked off her clunky waitress shoes and lifted a foot into her lap to rub her aching arch.

The television emitted her mother's soap opera at full volume. Immy dully watched a heartbroken man pleading with a bleached blonde to take him back. It cut to an even louder commercial for hair coloring. Immy reached over and snatched the remote from the arm of the recliner and clicked the damn thing off, waiting for Mother's slow return. She wasn't rushing now, it seemed. Immy's elbow knocked her mother's glass of iced sweet tea to the carpet.

Now I'll hear it. Her precious sweet tea and her precious carpet.

The tea sank into the thin gray mat that her mother vacuumed every day to within an inch, no, to within a millimeter of its life. When the green plaid couch and recliner had been new and the carpeting thicker, they had looked distinguished in the dark paneled room. Sort of British, Immy had thought back then. She had always loved this room and still did.

Feeling the floor shake from her mother climbing the porch steps, she got up, straightened her shoulders, and prepared to face her consequences. She had to decide if she should tell the whole truth, too. Or if she dared.

Hortense, out of breath from her unaccustomed exertion, yanked the door open and paused. After a few noisy pants, she managed to speak. "What is transpiring? You tell me that, little missy."

"Mother, close the door. The neighbors will hear." *Ha. That's what she always says to me.*

Hortense slammed it shut and folded her arms. "I am awaiting your response."

She makes me feel like I'm ten, dammit, but at least she's back to normal with her vocabulary. Immy lifted her chin. "I quit, I told you." Immy was proud that there was a little edge to her voice.

"Why?" Hortense asked, with a puzzled, pained look. Her mother hadn't raised her to be a quitter.

That knot was taking over her insides. Immy wanted to double over. Lying to Uncle Huey was one thing, but she wasn't sure she could get used to standing up to Mother. Even with the door closed, the neighbors were getting an earful through the thin metal walls.

Immy glanced at the air to her left for an answer. What would sound plausible?

"He asked me to put in double shifts again next week."

"Working extra hours would not be injurious to your person or to your pocketbook, Imogene."

This wasn't going to fly. Immy focused over her mother's right shoulder and pulled a better reason, she hoped, out of thin air, or rather, borrowed it from the goings on at the diner earlier. "I'm so sick and tired of him pinching my bottom."

"What? You're ... he ...." Hortense deflated, unfolding her arms and stumbling across the living room to take the seat Immy had vacated. She didn't notice the spilled ice tea.

Her little fib was shocking Mother more than she had thought it would. Immy hadn't even thought Mother would believe her. Did Hortense really think her own husband's brother would pinch Immy's bottom? The brother of her own dead, sainted husband?

"Uncle Huey is … is a dirty old man?" Hortense must have been so shocked she couldn't think up a big word for creep. She looked older than she had a moment before. Her thinly plucked eyebrows furrowed upwards toward a mass of curly gray hair, the curls compliments of Cathy's Kut and Kurl on Second Street.

"Yes." Another big sigh. "Uncle Huey is a filthy, dirty, lecherous …"

"I get it." She waved her hand for Imogene to stop. "Enough adjectives."

"He's always hit on the waitresses." *That much, at least was true.* "I've told him over and over to keep his hands off." *I'm getting in deep. Maybe I should tell her the real reason I quit, but how can I?* The lie was gaining momentum, taking on a life of its own. Immy had a sour taste in her mouth.

"Why have you never told me this? How could he? This is the family's business. He's impugning the honor of your dead father, your dear, sainted father." Immy mouthed the last words with her.

Hortense shook her head and stared at the spreading tea stain, still not seeing it. Immy's father had owned half the restaurant when he was alive. Hortense wasn't the only one who wished he were still here. In fact, Immy kept his detective badge in her top dresser drawer and got it out often to rub her fingers over the shiny surface. He was the reason for her dream. His had failed. Hers would not.

Imogene watched her mother process the information, then come to a conclusion. Not a good one, she could tell.

Hortense caught the fabric of her polyester pants in a clenched fist. "I'll tear his damn puny testicles off." Her voice was soft, almost gentle. Bad sign. "I will remove them from his insignificant torso and I will cram them down his damn throat."

The sour mass in Immy's stomach doubled. That's what she got for telling whoppers. Then her stomach clenched still another notch.

"Mother, where's Drew?" Immy's daughter was usually home from pre-school by now. How could she not have noticed? What kind of a mother was she?

"They had a field trip today. They'll be home late." Immy would have known that, if she'd read the note Drew brought home. Hortense always read them, though. She also picked Drew up from daycare, since Immy worked until after their pick-up time. Until today. "The school said they'd drop the kids off at the house around five." Her fleshy face grew grimmer. "Huey, you no good …"

Hortense heaved herself up from deep in the couch and lumbered out of the room, gathering momentum as she marched out the door a second time and careened down the stairs.

Immy pressed her stomach where it ached and considered her options. Her daughter was not a concern for a couple of hours, Mother had said.

A third big sigh. *Better stop doing that or I'll hyperventilate.* Immy pulled her shoes back on, donned her sweater, and cracked the door open after a discreet interval.

Mother was going at a fast waddle down the road. Uncle Huey was in for a tongue-lashing, but since he'd never pinched Immy's bottom, Huey wouldn't know why the hell Hortense was screaming at him. Maybe Immy should hear what went on in case she needed to defend her lie to Mother or step up and confess.

She would tail Mother. She needed the practice anyway. Immy entered the place in her head where she existed not as Imogene Duckworthy, overeager but sometimes ineffectual unwed parent of Drew, nor as the smothered only daughter of her doting but critical mother, nor as a clumsy waitress — no, none of these. In this nice place, where her stomach never hurt, Imogene was Detective Duckworthy, a daughter her father would have been proud of, but one whose existence her mother would prevent if she could.

She watched until Hortense disappeared around the corner of the last trailer on the block. Then Immy dashed outside and ran in the opposite direction to get to the diner by another route. She could beat her mother there and hide in the doorway of the library next door. Would Mother really harm Uncle Huey? She sure did look mad enough to spit. Maybe madder. It worried Immy a little. She needed to keep track of what was going on.

She hadn't been honest with Uncle Huey, nor with Mother, because her dream was too fragile to take the ridicule she expected. When she made it come true, they would all sit up and take notice. She hoped.

For now, Immy had no idea what to do about the situation. She hoped Detective Duckworthy would know.

Two

Immy pressed herself tightly into the narrow doorway of the library. It was shallow but deep enough to hide her thin form. Her foot stuck when she tried to move it out of sight. Some jerk had spit gum on the sidewalk, right outside the library.

I wonder if that's where the term gumshoe comes from, hiding in dirty alleys and getting gum on your shoes.

She scraped it off on the shallow step as best she could, then ducked back as she spied her mother sailing down the sidewalk, pink windbreaker flapping behind her like the wake of an ocean liner. She heard Hortense rattle the knob, then bang on the door of the diner. It wasn't open for supper on Mondays, so it was closed down now until tomorrow, no doubt locked. Uncle Huey was most likely upstairs doing his books. Clem, the cook, was probably in the back, chopping vegetables and making gravy for tomorrow. Baxter should be around, washing dishes or cleaning up. If Immy still worked there, she would be in the dining room right now, refilling salt shakers and ketchups and wrapping forks and knives into paper napkin bundles.

Hortense kept pounding, and eventually the door opened, then slammed shut. Immy peeked out. Her mother had entered the restaurant. How would a detective operate in this situation? She had no idea. She would have to get a book on the subject of being a PI next time she went to the book store in Wymee Falls. There were no PI books in the library, Immy knew, because she had read every book of crime fiction and mystery it held. If picking up her new business cards hadn't taken longer than she'd thought it would, she would have looked for one today. Surely someone had written a guide for PIs, one of those

Dummy or Idiot things. She had read one of those on child care once, and it had seemed pretty good.

For now, she craned her neck out of her cubbyhole to search the sidewalk for onlookers. She didn't want anyone to see that she was spying on her own mother. Next to Huey's Hash, on the corner, stood the video rental place with the huge plate glass windows. No one was there at the moment. The library, where she hid, had closed at noon, since it closed early three days a week due to budget cuts. Beyond the library was the tiny hardware store, its pale yellow paint peeling from the west Texas sun. No one was outside.

There was a time, Mother often said, when Saltlick seemed destined for greater things, like an unlimited budget and possibly a real stoplight on Second Street instead of the yellow, blinking one. The town had swelled years ago with the booming oil industry, specializing in providing drilling equipment for wildcatters; but as the drilling subsided, and the speculators moved on to natural gas, Saltlick sank as well. At the edge of town remained one last equipment yard, half-full of rusting pipes and pumps. Somehow, though, the town and the people hung on. They were from tough stock.

Across the street from the library and hardware store stood the All Sips "inconvenience store," as Hortense called it, with its gas pumps. Next to that, directly across from the diner, was the popular Cathy's Kut and Kurl, painted a vivid, sickening pink. No one was in sight there either. She waited a few more minutes, gathering her courage, then made her move.

Immy slunk to the door of the restaurant and peered in through the glass. The dining room was dark and empty. The chairs, flipped onto the tabletops, stuck their legs toward the whitewashed ceiling. The Closed sign was flipped out, but Immy was in luck. The door was unlocked. Huey must have forgotten to lock it after he let Hortense in.

Immy slipped inside, quiet as a possum, clicked the door shut behind her, and had no trouble telling where they were.

Shouts rained down from the upstairs office. She peeked into the kitchen but didn't see the cook, Clem, or Baxter, the handsome devil of a busboy, either. Clem was probably in the storeroom. From the looks of the half-chopped cabbage head, he was in the middle of making coleslaw. He had also finished dry mixing the biscuits for tomorrow as evidenced by the liberal sprinkling of flour on the floor. Sometimes he sent Baxter out to get supplies, so maybe that's where he was.

"You are out of your fucking mind!" That was Uncle Huey's unmistakable nasal tenor. And his language.

"Don't you speak to me like that. I know my daughter wouldn't prevaricate to me!"

Immy flinched. *Not usually, but …*

"She just did! I have never touched her, never!" *OK,* prayed Immy, *let's drop this subject right now.*

"Then why did she quit?"

Immy held her breath and listened for the answer. It came, softer than the preceding shouting match. She had to move closer to the bottom of the stairs to hear. Huey told Hortense that Immy had quit because he demanded she work extra shifts this coming weekend.

"You're a filthy, rotten liar!" The volume was going up again. "Imogene Duckworthy is not afraid of a little hard work. Thank the good Lord above she takes after her father, bless his soul, and not you. You're a bum, nothing but a bum. You always were a bum, and you always will be."

Huey's voice got very quiet, but Immy could make out what he said. "Leave my office right now." He bit off his words and sounded mucho ticked off.

"Not until you tell me what you did to her!"

"I'll call the cops if you're not out of here in two minutes. One, one thousand, two, one thousand …"

Immy heard her mother's muttered curse, then her heavy tread sounded on the wooden floor above, heading for the stairs.

Immy fled out the door and ran around the corner, and she kept running until she was home. Her mother didn't return for hours, long after Drew was dropped off from her field trip.

THAT EVENING IMOGENE WAS SITTING on the carpet in front of the TV playing Candy Land with her daughter, Nancy Drew Duckworthy, commonly called Drew, when her mother muted the television, directed a glare in her direction, and started in on her. Immy had know this was coming and braced herself, hunching her shoulders toward the game board.

"You know, Huey says he never pinched your bottom."

"Mother, not in front of ..." Immy nudged her head toward tender young Drew, whose ears would have stood up if she had been a dog. Why couldn't her mother have said *gluteus maximus* or some such?

"Unca Huey pinched Mommy?" Drew squealed, glee behind her sparkling green eyes.

"Drew," said Immy, trying to sound as authoritative as her mother always did, "go to your room and bring me your Fuzzy Bear."

"Why?"

Hortense took over. "Do it, Drew. Now." There, that authoritative sound. Why did her own voice have to be so high-pitched?

"OK, Geemaw." Drew scooted down the hallway, her bright chestnut curls bouncing behind her.

"I'm waiting." Hortense drummed her fingers against her ample thigh.

A knock on the front door interrupted them.

Saved by the bell. Or the knock, since we don't have an operating doorbell.

Hortense aimed her annoyance at the door and nodded for Immy to get it.

Immy jumped up gladly. *I hope it's a SWAT team that picked the wrong house to search for a meth lab. That might, just might, make Mother forget about this.*

It was almost as good. In the doorway stood a small man, dwarfed by a huge white box. He thrust it toward Immy. A delivery van from a Wymee Falls florist idled on the front yard grass.

"For Mrs. Duckworthy," he announced.

"I'm Mrs. Duckworthy." Hortense pushed past her daughter and grabbed the box. She tore it open, and it revealed a mound of lush, de-thorned red roses.

"Wow," breathed Immy. "How many are there?"

"Twenty-four," answered the little delivery man with pride.

Drew ran into the room carrying a Barbie doll. "Drew," said Immy, "I thought I told you to get Fuzzy Bear."

"Don't like Fuzzy Bear. Like Barbie."

Immy shuddered. She didn't want to raise a Barbie-loving daughter. That doll sent all the wrong messages to children, for heaven's sake. She reached to take the doll, but Drew snatched it back, gave an impish grin, and ran down the short hallway to the bedroom that mother and daughter shared.

"Imogene, compensate the man." Hortense carried the flowers into the kitchen. Immy found a dollar in her purse and reluctantly parted with it. There weren't that many more where it came from. She hoped Uncle Huey would pay her soon for the shifts she had worked before she quit.

She wandered into the kitchen. Her mother was on her knees, rummaging under the sink. Hortense emerged triumphant with her one and only cut glass vase. Immy gave her mother a hand up and helped her trim the stems. The blossoms looked crowded in the vase, but Hortense said she didn't want to put them in plastic.

"Who are they from?" asked Immy, although she already knew. Clem Quigley, the cook at Huey's Hash, was the only person who regularly sent Hortense flowers.

Hortense opened the florist's square envelope and held the card to her bosom, smiling. "Such a silly, old fool," she said, but she kept smiling.

The subjects of bottom pinching and lying to your mother didn't come up again that night.

The next morning, as Immy drove the family behemoth, an ancient Dodge van of bilious green, into Wymee Falls, she worried that her lies were piling up a little too tall, like tumbleweed stacked up against a fence by the wind.

She had told her mother she was going to the larger town to look for work in some restaurants, which wasn't too much of a lie. She was looking for work, but not waiting tables. That was a dead end for her.

Why hadn't she shown her mother the business cards she'd picked up yesterday? Maybe she should have. No, she argued, she'd better not. If she did, her mother would completely dismiss her desire to open her own business, she knew she would.

She knew the litany by heart, having heard it often enough. Little Immy couldn't do anything on her own. The family took care of her. Look how she had become an unwed mother at eighteen. She hadn't graduated from high school with honors and become a librarian like her brilliant mother.

But she had graduated, in spite of being pregnant when she crossed the stage. She wasn't stupid, and she would prove it. She did not have to be taken care of.

Whenever Immy mentioned wanting to be a detective, Mother told her she needed to think realistically, but Immy had known for years that she could detect. Hadn't she found the Yarborough twins' new puppy when it was missing? She had been the one to leave the gate open while feeding it for them when they were dove hunting, that was true, but she had followed the little puppy footprints in the dust beside the road, discovered it under a clump of sagebrush, and brought it home safe and sound.

She had also found out why old Mrs. Jefferson couldn't hear her chiming clock any longer. One reason, of course, was that Mrs. Jefferson had become almost stone deaf. In trying to insert a new battery, the lack of which was the reason for the non-chiming, Immy managed to mangle the chiming mechanism so that it would remain non-chiming forever. But Mrs. Jefferson would never know, unless she got a new hearing aid, and she thought Immy had fixed it.

Those were her two most successful cases, but she was confident there would be others.

She'd been poring over the classified want ads in the paper that came to the diner for the last several weeks, and today she had her route mapped out. Although, she thought, Wymee Falls wouldn't be hard to find your way around, even if you hadn't grown up twenty miles from it. It was a town holding its breath, in her mind, waiting for the next big industry to move in, hanging on, sort of like Saltlick but on a slightly larger scale. It had multiple restaurants, but most of them were steak places with a few chains. It had a shopping center, but one of the two anchor stores had moved out ten years ago. It had quite a few strip shopping centers, but only about two-thirds of them were occupied. When the interstate planners had decided to bypass the town with the superhighway, hope for vast expansion in the near future had been shelved. The citizens of Wymee Falls, the optimistic ones, like commercial real estate agents, still held out hope for the far future.

Her first stop in the city was a small, dark office downtown. It was on one of the main streets, and Immy had to park on a side street. Half the block was a bus stop, and three extra-long-bed pickups took up the four parking spaces. Wymee Falls needed some parking garages. The private investigator proprietor had advertised for an office assistant, but he wasn't in, and the place was locked up tight. Maybe she should have called first, but this was a spur-of-the-moment trip, after all. Immy slipped her résumè under the door. She hoped that working at this place would teach her how to open up her own place.

Next, she drove to the Wymee Falls police station located at the edge of the downtown area. It had a parking lot, Immy was glad to see. She walked in and applied for the advertised job of dispatcher. Not today, and not next month, but one day she was going to be handing out her own business cards, once she learned the ropes a little, and one of these jobs would help. She hoped.

After she filled out the form and was told she would be called for an interview, she visited the used book store, a cramped, cheerful place on a shady, unzoned side street. It was an old house that had been converted to a shop. She found an almost new copy of *The Moron's Compleat PI Guidebook*, from the Moron's Compleat Guidebook series. Just what she needed! She thumbed through the pages, eager to devour the entire volume. She clutched it to her chest and paid for it, then carefully put it on the floor of the van.

To make it seem to Mother like she was job hunting all over Wymee Falls, she drove around for a while before returning home. It was surprising more jobs weren't being offered in her field. The job market was bad, but weren't people always looking for answers to life's puzzles?

That afternoon, while her mother picked Drew up from preschool, Immy took advantage of being alone to leaf through her new book.

She had just finished studying the table of contents and had almost decided which section to read first when a hard rap sounded on the door. Immy peeked out the window in the door to see the Saltlick Police Chief, Emmett Emersen, in full uniform and wearing a nasty scowl on his beefy face.

She opened the door. "Can I help you?"

He strode in and looked around. "Where's your mother?"

"She's picking Drew up. What do you need?" Why was Emmett acting so serious? Solemn, almost. He usually cracked a lame joke out the window when she saw him driving around in his shiny new Saltlick cop car, one of two the small town owned. He drove the new one, and the other policeman got the old one.

"She'd better be back soon."

Immy stood rooted to the spot while Emmett paced the length of the small room and back. Something was very wrong.

Emmett paced out to the front porch to wait, and Immy followed. Hortense soon pulled the old Dodge up beside the trailer. Immy wanted to warn her about Emmett's mood but couldn't move, couldn't get her mind in gear to figure out how.

Drew ran up the steps to her mother and gave her a hug. Immy thought to tell Drew to go to her room before Emmett could confront Hortense. For once Drew didn't tell Immy she couldn't make her do it.

"Hi Emmett," began Hortense with a smile. Then she saw his stormy visage. "Do you want to come in?" Her voice wavered a bit as her smile faded. Emmett trailed Hortense and Immy into the living room.

"Uh, please have a seat." Hortense plopped down in her recliner, leaving the plaid couch for Immy and the chief to share. Immy perched as close to the arm as she could. Emmett laid his shiny-billed hat on the cushion between them.

"I have a few questions." He pulled a curling notebook from his pocket and clutched a pen in his thick fingers. "Where were you yesterday, late afternoon and evening?"

"Mostly here," answered Hortense. "Why?"

He turned to Immy. "Where were you?" His ruddy complexion was at its ruddiest. Immy even saw his scalp redden through his thin gray-blond hair.

Immy tried to swallow, but a huge lump was in the way. She licked her lips with an almost dry tongue. She twisted her straight reddish-brown hair around a shaky finger. This was scary, being questioned by a crabby police chief. How much to tell?

"I worked part of my shift at the diner, then I came home."

"When did you come home?"

"Um, it was about—what was it, Mother? About one?"

"Closer to two, I should think." Hortense didn't look at her daughter, keeping her gaze intently on the chief.

Actually it was around three. My shift went until five and I quit three hours early. Then picked up my new business cards. If Mother weren't here I could tell him the actual time I quit, but I don't want to make her look like a liar.

"And neither of you were in the restaurant later than that?"

"Most certainly not," blurted Hortense. She stiffened her spine and sat as tall as her five feet, two inches permitted. "I never go there anymore. I do not like the way Hugh manages the establishment." She shook her head, setting her chins quivering.

Yikes! Mother is lying to the police on purpose! Now what do I do?

"Why do you ask, pray tell?" Hortense said.

Mother, maybe you shouldn't be so belligerent with the cops.

"Were either of you there today at any time?"

They both shook their heads. *At least we don't have to lie about that. We haven't been near there all day. Mother's only gone out to take Drew to playschool and pick her up. I think.*

Why was the chief looking at them like that? Immy felt her neck hairs rising.

"Hugh Duckworthy was found murdered this morning. Someone gagged him to death. A package of raw sausage was stuffed down his throat."

Three

After the chief left their home, Immy tried to get used to the fact that Hugh was dead, to wrap her head around the idea. It didn't quite seem real. Such a short time ago, he had been alive. And she had parted with him on bad terms. At some point, she knew she would have to deal with that, but she didn't want to now.

Hortense was quiet, too, and seemed a little jumpy. It had to be as big a shock to her as it was to Immy.

Immy shook herself to try to get rid of the image of Huey lying dead with raw sausage protruding from his mouth. Ugh. The chief said it was thawed when they found him but had probably been frozen when Hugh died, judging from the abrasions and the fact that the wrapper was ripped mostly off.

Maybe she should try some deduction to take her mind off the vision. That's what a PI would probably do. Hugh always kept his supply of sausage in the freezer until he was ready to use it. If it was thawed when his body was discovered and frozen when he died, the murder must have happened well before he was discovered. There! That was good deduction, she felt.

The busboy had found Hugh when he arrived at the diner that morning, Emmett had said. The busboy was probably Baxter. The last Immy knew, Kevin, the other busser, had the week off and was visiting family in Abilene.

"Mother, where were you yesterday after you went to the diner?"

Her mother looked more worried than Immy had ever seen her.

"I just walked for a while. Hugh had me so upset. He said you were lying to me about the reason you quit. I didn't know what to think. You don't usually lie to me." She didn't look at Immy. If she had, Immy might have had to avoid her gaze. "I went to the little park on the other side of town and sat on a bench. I must have stayed there a long time. My feet started feeling numb. It was cold out and windy."

How to say this to her own mother? "Mother, why did you lie to the police chief?"

"I was embarrassed when he first asked me. I didn't want Emmett to know how foolishly I had behaved, storming over there and ranting away at Hugh like that. But Immy, Huey's dead. Murdered. Now Emmett might think I did it."

"Why would he think that?" *Should I think it, too?*

Hortense spotted the book lying beside Immy. "What's that?" Her voice took on an accusatory tone.

Good save. Way to change the subject, Mother. "It's something I picked up the other day."

Hortense snatched it from the couch. "'*The Moron's Compleat PI Guidebook*? Why the hell do you have this?"

"I bought it." Immy stuck her chin out. She wasn't going to back down on her dream. "And I bought these." She fished her new business cards out of her purse and waved them in front of her mother. This had the effect that a rodeo clown with flapping arms has on a bull.

Hortense read from a card. "Imogene Duckworthy, PI. PI, for God's sake?"

"Mother, your language."

"Don't you Mother-your-language me, little missy. PI? You are not a damn PI. You are not going to have anything to do with investigation or detective work of any kind. Get that through your substantially thick cranium. Your dead sainted father, bless his soul, was a detective, and that's what got him killed."

"He was a police detective. There's a big difference. I want to be another sort of detective."

Hortense read from the card. "No case too big or too small. We do it all." She glared at Immy. "Imogene Duckworthy, you are not Nancy Drew. You are not even Agatha Christie, and you are not a detective." She flung the cards down and threw the book on top of them, then stomped to her bedroom and slammed the door.

Immy knelt and gathered her belongings, blinking back her tears. She knew Mother wanted the best for her, but she didn't understand Immy's passion. *I will not cry. Detectives don't cry. She will not make me. There's no reason I can't be a detective. I don't know how yet, but I will some day. I swear to God above I will.*

Four

The next morning Immy saw Emmett Emerson pull into the yard as she returned from dropping Drew at preschool. Drew had wanted to take one of her Barbies to school today, and Immy had decided it was time to put her foot down. She had won, too. Immy knew she should be stricter with Drew, but Hortense did a good job of keeping Drew in line.

On the short trip back she had paid scant attention to her driving, proceeding on automatic pilot. She imagined instead what furnishings her office would have, wondering how and when she would get herself an office and where it would be. Not here in Saltlick. Not enough business in such a tiny town. Most likely Wymee Falls. She didn't want to get too far from home.

Hortense appeared on the front porch, frowning down at the chief's car. It must have just pulled up, because the chief was still in the driver's seat, and the door was just opening.

Immy grabbed the offending Barbie from the car seat and climbed out to put herself between the chief and her mother. Emmett nodded at Immy as he got out of his vehicle but didn't smile. He turned to Mother, looking through Immy.

"Hortense, Officer Ralph just let me know what Cathy from over to the Kut and Kurl told him yesterday. I'm gonna have to ask you some more questions."

"Pertaining to what?" Gosh, Mother sounded belligerent. "Immy, you can go inside."

There Mother went again, treating Immy like a child. Immy complied, though, stomping up the steps to make her point. She pulled the drape aside a couple inches and peeked out the window to watch them.

They spoke a few quiet words, then Hortense climbed into the chief's car.

Immy watched the shiny Saltlick cruiser disappear around the corner. Emmett was driving, but her mother was in the back seat. Immy clutched the thin drape at the window as she staggered back. The curtain rod clattered to the floor.

Was Hortense being arrested for Huey's murder? If not, why take her away in the back seat? If anyone saw her, and you can bet someone would in this town, it would look like she was being treated like a common criminal.

Think, Immy, think. Think like a detective.

Immy tried to marshal her jumbled thoughts. The chief had said Huey was found dead yesterday morning, but he had asked them where they'd been the afternoon before. The afternoon before was when Immy had quit and when Hortense had gotten into a screaming match with Huey, then lied about.

This raised several questions. When had Huey been killed? They must think it happened that afternoon. That matched the thawed sausage evidence. Had Emmett found out her mother lied? Had someone seen her at Huey's Hash? What on earth had Cathy said to Ralph, the other officer?

But the main question was, how could Immy convince the chief that her mother had not killed Uncle Huey? She wouldn't let herself think of the possibility that her own mother had done it. Could Immy cast suspicion on someone else? Was anyone else being questioned? Had Emmett investigated Clem, the cook, or the busboy, or the other waitress? This town was too small for all of that questioning to go unnoticed. Gossip should be flying. Maybe it was flying, and she hadn't heard it. She hadn't been out today except to drop Drew off.

After Immy put the drape back up, she got her jacket on and got ready to do some real, live detective work. She snatched the pad of paper and pen by the house phone in case she needed to take notes. The pad was an order pad from the diner, she noticed. They used to come home in her pockets often. A shiver ran up her spine at the unbidden thought of Uncle Huey dead, murdered.

Before she could get out the door, her cell phone rang. A raspy-voiced man told her he was Detective Mallett, Mike Mallett.

"You applied for a job at my office?"

Immy held her breath. Was this her big break? "Yes? I mean, yes, I did."

"Your paperwork looks good. If you still want the job, I'd like to do an interview next week, say, ten o'clock Wednesday?"

A scream tried to escape her throat, but she strangled it until after she had hung up.

"Yes, yes, yesss! I'm working in a PI's office. Yes!" She pumped her hands skyward toward her ascending fortunes.

Now, should she tell her mother? Hortense probably wouldn't take it well. Immy would decide later about when to tell her—and exactly what.

As she fired up the van she wondered just where she was going to go to investigate, but when she cruised down Second Street, the main artery of Saltlick, the van seemed to know what to do. It nosed into the curb in front of Cathy's Kut and Kurl. A glance at the clock told her it was after nine-thirty. The shop should be open now.

Yellow tape festooned the door of Huey's Hash across the street. How could such a bright, happy color look so gloomy?

The Pepto Bismol pink exterior of Cathy's lent a festive gaiety to the block, though. Immy pushed through the glass door with its tinkling bell and asked Cathy if she had time to do a shampoo. That was the cheapest thing Immy could think of on the spur of the moment as a cover for her inquisition.

"Sure, honey, not too busy this time of day. C'mon back." Cathy, rail thin with bleached white straw on her head where most people had hair, scurried to the back room and motioned Immy to a seat in front of the first of her three black sinks. Immy sat, and Cathy ran a quick brush through Immy's straight locks, whipped a plastic cape around her shoulders, tilted her onto the spongy sink lip, and sprayed her head with scalding water.

"What's goin' on with that mama of yours, Immy?"

"What do you mean?" She had read in her PI guidebook that answering questions with questions elicited information from informants.

"Well, that po-liceman Ralph, you know, that big deputy or somethin', came around and axe me if I seen her day before yesterday. You know, Ralph? That ex-jock. Kinda cute."

Of course she knew Ralph. Everyone did. Immy shivered under Cathy's strong fingers, which were digging into her scalp. Another question, she reminded herself. "What did you tell him?"

"I tole him what I seen."

Another tactic Immy had read about was that of remaining silent. Suspects, the book said, will sometimes give information to fill the gaps in conversation. So she tried that next. She closed her eyes and kept her mouth shut. It worked.

"Your mama went in there and then ran out like a bat outta hell not fifteen minutes later. Then Hugh was found dead the next day." Cathy's fingers gouged into Immy's scalp harder. "I didn't know what to think, but I hadda tell him. I'm sure Hortense wouldn't hurt a fly, but I hadda tell Ralph. He's the po-lice."

Somehow, Immy kept her eyes closed and kept from flinching under Cathy's death grip massage. Had Cathy seen her in the doorway of the library or entering the diner? She would say so if she had, wouldn't she?

"That floozy waitress, what's her name?" said Cathy.

"Xenia?" Xenia Blossom was the one who had quit the same day Immy did, in the morning, the one who actually had quit because Uncle Huey pinched her bottom.

"Yeah, her and that gangster-lookin' boyfriend of hers was there a little before your mama was. They left like they was all steamed up about somethin'."

"Do you know if Ralph talked to anyone else?"

"Can't say I do."

"You see any other cars or people there yesterday?" Immy cringed, waiting for the answer to include herself.

"Nope. I was back and forth from front to back all afternoon."

So if Xenia was there before her Mother, Xenia and Frank, her boyfriend, hadn't killed Uncle Huey. She had heard Hortense and Huey arguing with her own ears. He had been alive when Mother was there. *Mother,* Immy thought, *made a big mistake lying to Emmett like that. I wonder how much trouble she's in. Why in the hell did she lie to him if she didn't kill Huey?*

Half an hour later Immy left the shop with clean, shiny hair and no idea where to go next. Maybe she should talk to Huey's longtime cook Clem. The diner, directly across the street from Cathy's, was closed indefinitely, of course, with that yellow tape stretched across the doorway, but through the alleyway between the buildings Immy spied dark metal behind the diner. She crossed the street and walked around to the back. Sure enough, Clem's dark blue pickup was parked beside the dumpster bin. She was a little surprised. What would he be doing there today? On the other hand, Clem had practically lived at the place for many years now, spent most of his waking hours there on a normal day, which today wasn't.

Yellow tape hung down one side of the back door, not fastened to the other jamb. Had Clem pulled it down to get in? At any rate, she wouldn't be trespassing if the tape was down, she reasoned. She pulled her jacket sleeve over her hand and, protecting the knob from her fingerprints, tried it. The door swung open.

"Clem?" she called softly. The lights in the back hallway were off, but a strip of brightness showed beneath the door to the kitchen. "Clem?"

She knocked lightly on the kitchen door, not wanting to startle him.

His gruff voice answered her. "Who the hell is it?"

Immy cracked the door open and showed her face. "It's me, Clem. I wanted to see if you were all right." The familiar smells of the diner drifted into the hallway, but they were old, stale odors. No cooking was going on today.

He perched on his stool at the counter where he usually made out the menus for the week, but no menus were in sight, just an empty countertop. What was he doing here?

"What do you mean?" he said. "Why shouldn't I be all right? You mean the stolen stuff?"

He didn't exactly look all right. His large, puppy dog eyes were troubled, and his jowls seemed to droop more than usual.

"Well, I mean with Uncle Huey being dead and the restaurant being closed."

"Yeah. Damn shame about Hugh."

"I know he wasn't your favorite person." Immy leaned her elbows on the cool countertop, lacking another stool, and contemplated Clem across its broad, shiny, stainless steel surface. Clem would be a good match for Hortense in a contest for who weighed the most. His Santa Claus cheeks didn't glow with their normal ruddiness, but maybe that was because he wasn't standing over a stove or a grill. Those dewlaps of his swung as he slowly shook his head.

"What do you mean about stolen stuff?" asked Immy.

"Didn't you hear? There was a robbery when Hugh was killed. Hugh's wallet got stolen and all the cash from the safe. Damn thief even took the new shipment of sugar packets. Several boxes, too. If that don't beat all." He shook his head again. "I wasn't here right then, by the way."

"No, I didn't hear anything was stolen." So maybe a robber killed Huey? Taking the cash and the wallet made sense, but sugar packets? Maybe Clem was mistaken about that.

"It was nice of you to send flowers to Mother yesterday."

"Oh, hell, she deserves 'em. Her and me both hate what Hugh's done to this place. You remember when it was the Duckworthy Diner, when your grandparents ran it?"

"Just faint, early memories, and I think I mostly remember pictures of my family that were taken here."

"The old Double D was a fine eating establishment. People came from all the towns around to eat at the Duckworthy place. Those were good times. When your pa and Hugh ran it together, it was still good. But when Louie left to be a cop, Hugh wasn't up to runnin' it himself."

Clem shook his head. "I always wondered if Hortense and I could run this place together or maybe another one somewhere else, but she always says she doesn't want to."

"Clem, she retired from the library. She's never worked in a restaurant."

"I know, I know, but we'd make such a good team." Clem's goofy grin, incongruous on his hangdog face, was testament to his longstanding pursuit of Immy's mother. He looked at the grease-splattered ceiling with a faraway look in his eyes. "What a woman."

Immy walked back toward the van, still in front of Cathy's Kut and Kurl, wondering if anyone else could be a suspect. She had to admit that she hadn't really grilled Clem. He was kind of mourning. It didn't seem polite.

A tall, slim man, dressed cowboy style in boots, hat, and belt, leaned against the door to her van as she approached.

"Baxter, how nice to see you." When would it not be nice to see Baxter? No one in Saltlick was as good looking as he was, for sure.

"Same here, Imogene." He shifted the toothpick in his mouth to the other side. "Hey, damn shame about your uncle."

"Thanks." Those dark eyes and that curly hair peeking out from under his cowboy hat brim made her pulse quicken as usual. He looked even better in street clothes than in his busboy apron, and he always looked pretty good in that, too.

"What's gonna happen to the place?" He moved closer, and she could feel the warmth of his body.

"What place?"

"The diner, of course. You gonna run it?"

"Baxter, I haven't even thought about that. Chief Emersen has Mother at the station." Her voice threatened to crack.

"Your mother? What for?"

Now why did I blurt that out? Damn those deep, dark eyes of his. "I'm not sure. He came by and picked her up a couple of hours ago."

"Probably just wants to ask her some questions about Hugh. I guess you and her are his closest relatives. Who owns the diner now, you?"

"Do police usually take people to the station just to ask them questions? And for two hours?"

Baxter squinted at her. "How would I know a thing like that?"

Immy stuttered a few words to the effect that she didn't know how he would know, sorry for asking. She yanked the van door open, backed out, and headed down the road, glad to escape his accusatory glare.

She hoped Baxter hadn't thought she was implying he'd had trouble with the cops, because she was pretty sure he had. Must have been something Hugh or her mother had said, maybe before he came to Saltlick.

Now where?

Maybe her PI guidebook would hold some answers.

Five

The pages of *The Moron's Compleat PI Guidebook* blurred. Reading it wasn't doing a good job of taking her mind off Mother. Immy, feeling comfy on the plaid couch, and guilty for doing so, kept trying to picture her at the police station. Immy herself hadn't been inside the building since her fourth grade field trip. It wasn't a place Hortense encouraged her to frequent, although Immy often wanted to drop in. She always thought she might feel closer to her father there.

Louis Duckworthy had worked for the Police Department of Wymee Falls for fifteen years, achieving the rank of Detective. Some people, Immy knew, thought he had what it took to become Chief eventually. His career and his life were both cut short during a robbery at what was then still called the Double D Diner.

He had dropped in to see his brother and shoot the breeze after his shift, as he often did before returning home to Hortense and their twelve-year-old daughter Immy. Huey had been making a vegetable run, and it was assumed that Louie had entered the kitchen to wait for him. Since it was after hours and the restaurant was closed, they also assumed he had let himself in through the back door with his key.

When Huey returned from his errands, he found the kitchen door locked and his brother, shot and bleeding, on the kitchen floor. Detective Duckworthy died later in the hospital. The money till and the safe were both empty. It was the night before Huey usually deposited the week's receipts, so the thieves netted themselves a tidy sum.

Since the back door, the kind that had to be secured with a key, had been relocked, and Louie's key was still in his pocket, police investigators assumed the robbers had an inside accomplice. Although the murdering thieves were apprehended, the inside helper was never identified.

Immy flashed from the vision she had always had of her father, bleeding on the kitchen floor of the diner, to a vision of Hugh, dead in the same exact place. She had, of course, never seen either her injured father or Hugh's body in that spot, but she had a good enough imagination.

If only she hadn't left Uncle Huey on such bad terms. He wasn't a horrible guy and had been decent to her. Immy always regarded him as a less vivid version of her father. Huey was average height, and her father had been over six feet. Huey had dull brown hair, but her father's had been the same shiny chestnut as Drew's and just as curly.

Uncle Huey had been so mean lately, though. He had yelled at Immy over every little thing, flaring up at the least little imperfection. In retrospect, she wondered if something had been bothering him. He was never a jovial person, but he wasn't too hard to get along with. Usually.

That last morning Immy had knocked a bin of flour onto the floor, and Huey had almost skyrocketed through the ceiling. Immy couldn't understand that, and it surprised her. It wasn't as if she had never done that before. She had spilled every condiment the diner owned at one time or another, and she always cleaned up her messes. That day was no exception. She had even watered the scraggly pot of parsley he kept on the windowsill in the dining room. The poor thing got western sun and dried out every other day, but Huey insisted it be kept in the window. Live plants make the place classy, he'd say.

Since Immy was pretty sure she was going to be getting a new job, Huey's request to work extra hours had been a good excuse to walk out. His twangy whine had followed her out the door. She would always remember that as their last encounter. What she would give to have a better last memory.

Immy looked up at the clock over the television. She had skipped lunch, and it would soon be time to pick up her daughter.

Six

Drew ran into the house, shedding her light purple jacket, as soon as Immy stopped the van.

Immy called after her. "Wait!" She hurried into the trailer. "Drew, just go potty and put your jacket back on."

"I don't want to."

"Let's not fight, Drew. This is important. Geemaw's in trouble at the police station."

"Did the pleece arrest her?"

Good question. She had been there all day. Was she being questioned all this time, or was she rotting in a jail cell? "Well, I'm not sure. We have to find out what's going on, Drew. Get your jacket back on, and we'll go see."

She had cased the joint earlier, just before she picked up Drew, and now Immy circled the police building twice. The air still held a nip as spring moseyed along, taking its time getting to Saltlick. She would be glad when they quit having to bother with jackets, and the grass greened up. The dry, brown ivy that climbed the side of the police station and rustled in the wind would soon turn glossy green. The station looked a lot better in the summer.

Crossing her fingers, she hoped her strategy was a good one. It might be better if Drew weren't with her, but that couldn't be helped. She hadn't been able to think of a plan all day. In fact, she had been expecting her mother to call for a ride home in the morning, then in the early afternoon. Now mid-afternoon was disappearing, and still no call. Wasn't an arrested person allowed one phone call?

Earlier, after aimlessly leafing through her PI Guidebook for hours, she had formulated a plan. It hadn't come from the book

but from a TV show she had seen about a jailbreak. The book
didn't have anything in it about jailbreaks.

The police station was a tidy, one-story brick building. The
grandest things about it were the double entry doors of thick
glass, surrounded by an attractive, light stone facing. Small
windows ran down one side of the building, the ones near the
rear heavily barred. Midway was a door. Immy eyed the barred
windows.

That's probably where Mother is, she thought, *in one of those
cells.* She pressed her lips together tight, determined to get her
mother out of stir.

She parked by the side door and sat in the car for a moment
wondering what she would find inside. She pictured her mother
a victim of police brutality, being manhandled while helpless in
handcuffs. Pictured her having her mug shot taken, having her
chubby fingers pressed into sticky fingerprint goo. Pictured her
writhing on the floor, being tased. She felt a shiver, light as a
tarantula, crawl up her spine.

"OK, Drew, let's go see Geemaw."

"She's arrested in there?" Drew threw her seatbelt off and
climbed out of her car seat. She looked eager to see the inside of
the station.

Immy took Drew's hand, maybe as much for her own feeling
of security as Drew's, walked around to the front, and pushed
through the doors.

She walked to the glass—probably bulletproof, or why
would it be there?—and asked the creamy-hued, overly made-
up woman behind it, whom she had known all her life, if she
could please see Hortense Duckworthy.

"I'll check. And who are you?" Hortense would have said her
drawl was mellifluous. Immy wondered if those bleached
eyebrows could go any higher.

"What do you mean, who am I? We went to school together,
kindergarten to twelve, Tabitha." *I didn't like you then any better,
either, Miss Cheerleader Homecoming Queen Football Team Floozy.*

"My mother is back there, and I want to see her." Drew jumped up and down trying to see. Immy reached down and lifted her to sit on the counter.

Tabitha, who had picked up an old-fashioned telephone receiver, slammed it down and stood. "Get her off there." Mellifluousness was gone.

Immy took a step back, even though the thick glass was between them. "OK, OK. She just wanted to see. You don't have to be so rude."

"Have a seat over there." Tabitha jabbed a finger toward the molded plastic chairs that lined the wall.

As they sat, Tabitha seemed to calm down. She resumed her call, keeping the two miscreants in sight of her narrowed eyes, lined in black and shadowed in powder blue. Immy set her jaw. Drew kicked the metal chair leg over and over. Grimy, well-thumbed magazines littered a small table, but Immy didn't want to touch them. The air hung stale.

Immy thought hard, then approached the guardian of the window again. Time to get her plan rolling. "My daughter needs to use a restroom," she said.

Tabitha didn't answer, but she must have summoned him somehow, because eventually Emmett's assistant Ralph appeared. He opened a door and motioned them to follow him.

Ralph had a big grin for them, probably for Immy herself, she thought. He'd been two years ahead of her in school and had always been a little sweet on her. He had been a football player, though, and she didn't hang around with that crowd. She was intimidated by people that big, except for Mother, and had never responded to his overtures. She didn't think Ralph had been in any of the accelerated classes she had been assigned to, but to this day, he still called her occasionally.

They trailed behind Ralph down the hallway and past a heavy door. The outside door on the side of the building, right where she had parked, stood across the hallway. Two doors away was a restroom marked Women.

This just might work, she thought, seeing how close the restroom was.

Immy paused outside the heavy door to peek through the small glass window, crisscrossed with embedded wire. Her mother slumped in a folding chair at a battered table. She looked exhausted, but she was alone. There were no visible bruises or lacerations. There could be hidden ones, though. There were torture methods that left no marks. Immy hoped she wasn't too late.

Ralph, fully uniformed and armed, loomed in the hallway while she and Drew entered the restroom. He was still there when they emerged. It seemed rude, even if he did give them a polite nod. He led them past the room that held Hortense just as the smoke alarms started shrieking.

Imogene held her breath. Now was when her plan would either work or not.

Ralph threw open the interrogation room door where Hortense was and ran toward the front. "Fire!" he yelled. "Follow me!" He ran fast for such a big guy.

Instead of obeying and following Ralph, Immy ran into the room and straight to her mother. Her plan was working. At first, Hortense wouldn't, or couldn't, get up. She must have been sitting there for hours in that hard chair.

She grabbed her mother's hand. Stupid Ralph. If the station were really burning out of control, he would have let her mother fry in here.

"Is that the fire alarm? Is there a fire?" Hortense gave her daughter a dazed look.

Immy had never seen her mother look so demoralized and bedraggled. "It's part of my plan to get you out of here, Mother, my plan to spring you."

"Darling," she whispered back, "they think I killed Hugh. I really think that they really think that." There was fear in her wide eyes.

Immy paused just a second to figure out her mother's syntax, then resumed her urging. "Quick, before they come back." Immy tugged Hortense to her feet and dragged her into the hallway. It was empty, but she could see people milling about in the front vestibule through the open door.

"This way," Immy urged.

Hortense shook her head to clear it, stood tall, and was suddenly energized. The three pushed through the side door, clambered into the van, and Immy sped away, avoiding the front of the building.

"Ah. It worked! The old fire-in-the-wastebasket trick."

"You set the fire?" Her mother looked at her in amazement.

See, I'm not so helpless. Not so stupid, either. Immy nodded and a big grin split her face. "Jailbreak! How cool is that?"

"Mommy." Drew's tiny voice piped from the back seat.

Immy turned to see her daughter's puckered brow and worried eyes. "It's all right, sweetie. Fasten your seat belt. Mommy and Geemaw are all right. Aren't we, Mother?" The last question was more for Drew's sake than her own.

"Where we going, Mommy?" piped Drew.

Immy felt her mother and her daughter looking at her.

"Well, what's the next part of your plan?" asked Hortense.

Seven

Immy drove straight out of Saltlick and came to the next small town, Cowtail. Her plan had only extended through the jailbreak, so now she was improvising.

"I think we'd better lay low somewhere until the heat blows over, Mother."

"Imogene, why are you talking like that? You sound like a character in an old movie. An old, terrible movie."

More like the old detective novels she had read, Immy thought. She loved the way those characters talked.

"Still," Immy said, "don't you think we ought to hide out? Where would they not think to look for us?"

Hortense stared out the van window. They wended down Cowtail's main street, Second Avenue, as opposed to Saltlick's main drag, Second Street. Hortense had often voiced to Immy her opinion of the unoriginality of the city founders of both towns who had used exactly two brain cells to name the streets.

At the far edge of town squatted a squalid little strip motel, fronted by a trash-filled, dry swimming pool and advertising itself as Cowtail's Finest. "That's a falsehood," said Hortense. "There's a nicer one at the other end of town. We just passed it."

"Then let's stay here." Immy turned the van onto the asphalt in front of the door marked Office at the end of the building and jumped out. "They won't look here, will they? I'll see if I can park around back."

Half the long, rectangular building's rooms faced the road, but the ones on the back side, away from the highway, faced a cow pasture and couldn't be seen from the main road. Immy booked one in the rear and hurried to move the van out of sight.

It didn't take long to move in, since they lacked luggage. Drew tested the bed by jumping on it. Hortense inspected the bathroom by sniffing it. The bed and the bathroom must have both passed their tests, because Drew turned her attention to the TV remote, and Hortense entered the bathroom to use it.

Immy stood at the foot of the double bed and thought hard, frowning at the worn carpeting. She caught one elbow and drummed her other fingers against the side of her face. She couldn't picture the three of them in the bed before her. Maybe they could get a rollaway cot from the office. For now, she fished her trusty *PI Guidebook* out of her purse and sank onto the bed to page through it and try to formulate the next step of her plan.

"I know you're wondering," said Hortense, emerging from the bathroom, "why I reinvented reality for Chief Emersen. If those towels were any thinner, you could use them for wrapping paper." She flapped her still damp hands and settled onto the other side of the bed from Immy, who felt it depress at least a foot.

"I wondered why you lied, yes," said Immy. "I know you went to the diner."

"I know you know I did. I saw you as I was arriving. You were trying to hide in the library doorway. Where were you when I exited?"

Why did her mother not ask her what she overheard? Maybe she didn't know Immy had entered the building while she was there. "I left. I saw you go in and I left."

"So you know I did not harm Hugh."

"Of course you didn't, Mother." *I hope you didn't. That's exactly what I'm so afraid of.*

"And you didn't either?"

Immy shook her head and turned away from her mother, burying her face in her book. Did her mother suspect that she had killed him? Had she lied to protect Immy? So she wouldn't have to say she saw her there? Or did Mother kill him? Was she asking these questions now to make sure Immy didn't see or hear the murder? This was her mother. Immy's head swam. Her mouth felt dry. She was going to refuse to believe her mother could have killed anyone.

THE BLUE NORTHER THAT HAD KEPT the temperatures down for the past week or so blew itself out during the night, enabling the sun to rise unencumbered by clouds. Daylight shot through the thin curtains at the window of Cowtail's Finest, Room 205, hitting Drew first. She had slept curled up beside her grandmother in the double bed, Immy taking the cot they had gotten delivered from the office.

Immy watched the light creep across her daughter's soft, lax face, suddenly loving every inch of her even more than she always did. They had all slept in their clothes and gone to bed without bathing. Drew had been delighted about not brushing her teeth, but living like this wasn't fair to her. It couldn't go on too long.

Immy hitched herself off the cot and tiptoed into the bathroom with her cell phone. Clem answered after several rings, just as she was about to give up.

"Clem?" she whispered. "Can you do me a favor?"

"Imogene! Where are you? What's the matter? Sore throat?"

"No, I'm whispering because everyone is sleeping."

"Have you seen the news today, Imogene? Is Hortense all right?"

Oh, no, had they made the news? "Why? What do you know?" *And enough with the questions! Someone say something!*

"They're looking for you, for you and Hortense."

"Is it the FBI? Scotland Yard? We're on the lam."

"You're on the what?"

"I need you to do me a favor, Clem. Can you watch Drew for me for a few days?" A roach scuttled across the tile floor and disappeared behind the toilet. She swallowed a shriek. It was only a small roach, but Immy was barefoot. She climbed onto the toilet seat.

"Sure. I guess I can take her to the restaurant with me. I was thinking I might try and open up today or tomorrow."

She wondered how on earth he could do that, and why, but right now she had to get something on her feet and something to whack the roach with.

"Bring her on over to the diner, Immy," he said." I'll be here all day even if I don't get it opened up. You want to come wait tables?"

"Are you crazy? We're wanted. You just said so. I'll bring her around the back in about an hour, two at the most. Don't tell anyone you talked to me."

Sitting on the cot, she pulled yesterday's dirty socks back on.

"Imogene Duckworthy." Mother was awake. "I am so fatigued I can barely open my eyes. I'm utterly exhausted. What are you doing, skulking about?"

"I'm not skulking, Mother, I'm trying to let you get your rest."

Drew bolted up. "I'm hungry." She began sobbing.

Immy sighed. "We'll get something to eat in a minute, sweetie. Mother, I just called Clem and asked him to watch Drew for a while until the heat's off."

"Quit speaking in that manner. You sound like an idiot. Why did you ask Clem?"

Why did she? "Well, I knew he'd do it." She knew he'd do anything if it involved Hortense or her relatives. The man was so besotted.

Immy picked up Drew, still sniffling, and headed out the door.

"And I don't think he'll rat us out."

She didn't wait to see her mother's reaction.

Eight

Hortense looked as wrung out as she said she was, so Immy left her mother in the room and bundled her daughter into the van. After snatching a Cowtail morning paper from the front desk in the motel office, she headed for Saltlick.

"Where are we going, Mommy?" asked Drew.

"Uncle Clem is going to watch you for a while." Clem wasn't really an uncle, but Immy had always called him that.

Drew pondered this for a moment. "Watch me do what?"

Immy knew she couldn't use the babysit word. Drew did not like to be referred to as a baby. "You're going to stay with him at the restaurant today. Won't that be fun?"

"Why will it be fun? Does he have Barbies?"

The damn Barbies again. Immy smiled as broadly as she could and deflected Drew from Barbie thoughts. "He might let you help in the kitchen. Wouldn't that be fun?"

"There aren't any Barbies at the restaurant." Immy's deflection didn't work.

The highway was bordered on both sides by grazing pastures. "Look, Drew, cows!"

Drew gave them a glance, then returned her attention to her Barbie's shoes, which would be the equivalent of hooker four-inchers if Barbie were full sized. Another deflection fell flat.

As they approached Saltlick, Immy wracked her brain to think of all the alternate routes she knew to the diner. She couldn't just brazen her way down Second Street in her own vehicle, being a wanted criminal and all. Deciding on one of the less-traveled routes, she took a barely paved road that left the highway a half mile outside of Saltlick and wound around the

Go Kart race track, which was one of the Friday night hot spots of the town when it wasn't football season.

The van meandered cautiously down alleys and through the grade school parking lot and finally arrived at the back door of the diner.

"Now we have to be very quiet, Drew," Immy said, unbuckling her daughter from her car seat in the alley.

"Why, Mommy?"

Immy searched for an answer. "The people at the library next door might be reading."

Drew gave her a doubtful look, probably figuring out that wasn't the real reason, but she remained silent for the short walk to the kitchen.

Clem jerked his head around when he saw them. He sucked in his breath and tightened his grip on the small cell phone in his massive fist.

"That's all I can tell you," he said into the phone and snapped it shut. He looked past Immy and Drew to the hallway. "Isn't Hortense with you? Is she all right?"

"She's fine, Clem, just tired today from all the excitement of yesterday, I think. She's resting."

His face relaxed a little. "Poor thing. It's on TV that the police are looking for her and for you, too, of course. What can I do?"

"You said you'd watch Drew, right?"

"But isn't there anything else I can do to help? Can I bring you some food? Is Hortense getting enough to eat?"

"We'll be fine, Clem." Immy crossed her fingers behind her back and hoped it was true.

Drew had already jumped onto Clem's stool. She reached into the box on the work counter and pulled out a handful of sugar packets, laying them out to form what looked like a Barbie bed. At least there wouldn't be a battle getting her to stay with him.

"Where are her spare clothes?" asked Clem.

"Spare clothes, right. I guess there is something you can do. We didn't get a chance to take any clothes with us. The heat was on our tail. Could you go to the house and get her some?"

"Sure can." He grinned at being able to be of service to his beloved's granddaughter.

"You know about the loose screen in the back kitchen window?"

"Sure do. I'll send Drew in through the window, and she can let me in through the door. Do you need me to cook something for you?"

This gave Immy pause. Clem didn't often offer to cook when he wasn't working. In fact, she had never known him to. Immy would love for Clem to bring them some of his wonderful chicken salad, but then he'd know the location of their lair. "I guess not. Please just make sure Drew gets fed. She hasn't had breakfast yet today. Hortense and I will be very grateful for that."

Clem beamed, glad to be of service.

"Clem, you didn't happen to notice anything that day, did you? The day of the, well ... Where were you around that time, the time Huey bought it?"

Clem frowned, looking like a troubled basset hound. All he needed was a pair of long ears. His were pretty large, but they didn't hang down. "I had left shortly before. I wasn't here when Hugh was killed." He fiddled with the cell phone, still in his mitt. "We were out of cabbage for the coleslaw. I had to drive into Wymee Falls."

"Hey, my pitcher! That's my school pitcher!" Drew pointed to the Saltlick newspaper Clem must have left on the counter.

Immy came to the stool and looked over her daughter's shoulder, then swallowed, feeling she had a wad of cud in her gullet. "Yes. It looks nice, doesn't it?"

"Does it say anything about me?" asked Drew. "Your pitcher is there, too, and Geemaw. Look, there's Geemaw." She poked each figure with her index finger as she identified them.

"Yes. We're all there, aren't we? You don't need to shout, Drew."

The headlines were not good: Local Duo on Crime Spree.

The article was worse: Hortense Duckworthy, who was being questioned in connection with the death of Hugh Duckworthy, local business owner, managed to set fire to the jail in Saltlick and flee from there yesterday afternoon. Her daughter, Imogene, may have assisted her in the crime. It is believed they have a child with them, Nancy Drew Duckworthy, Imogene's daughter and Hortense's granddaughter, who may be in danger.

"Who wrote this?" Immy tore her eyes away from the paper and paced the length of the kitchen and back. She couldn't resist reading the rest of the article, though, and returned to peer over Drew's shoulder again. The reporter hinted that Mrs. Duckworthy had been elevated to the level of suspect in her brother-in-law's death, along with Imogene, and the article warned everyone to be on the lookout for them. There was something else about child endangerment.

Child endangerment! She's my daughter. I'm not endangering her. Jeez!

"It's all lies, Immy," said Clem, "obviously." He must have read the whole article already.

"Yes, obviously."

After Clem and her daughter left in his truck to get Drew's clothes, Immy considered her next move. She had wanted to pursue a career that involved catching criminals, not a career of being one. She had never even contemplated a life on the run and wasn't at all sure what to do. She needed another book. That meant a visit to the book store in Wymee Falls.

The only thing she knew she couldn't do was show her face in public. Maybe she could concoct a disguise, scout the territory incognito. Would there be anything usable in the van? She opened the back passenger door and rummaged through the collected debris beside Drew's car seat. She found several Barbie shoes and one tiny cardigan. There was also a full-sized cardigan, very full-sized. It was her mother's and said size 3X on the tag. A woolen cap was left over from winter. It had been bought so that it would fit Drew now and for several years in the future, and it was quite stretchy. Immy found she could stuff all her hair up under it. With the huge sweater wrapped around her, maybe she could get by without being made if she kept her head down. But what if she had to look up? She needed something more.

She crawled back to the storage space in the rear and hit the jackpot, a pair of Groucho Marx glasses with a mustache that Clem had given to Drew. Immy returned to the front seat and tried them on. No, the mustache looked a little too plastic. She broke it off and tried the glasses again. Pretty good, unless you looked closely enough to see there were no lenses. It would have to do. She was a desperado, after all, and they are desperate people.

Immy drove into Wymee Falls and went straight to the book store. She parked in the alley behind it so no one would see her van. Maybe the police had her license number and had put out an APB, or maybe they used a BOLO. Either one would form a dragnet that might reel her in.

She walked to the front of the store with tiny steps, hunching her shoulders forward and keeping her head low. She hoped to look nearsighted. No one would be looking for a nearsighted person. Her eyesight was excellent, after all. Everyone knew that.

She knew she couldn't loiter. Her heart hammered as she zeroed in on the How To aisle and grabbed a book called *Criminal Procedures*, then picked up a copy of the Wymee Falls newspaper. When she paid at the front counter, she tried to fumble her money a little like an old person. That proved easy with the way her hands shook. She didn't dare look up to see how her disguise was going over. She handed over the money, glad she still had enough left for a few more days, picked up the book and the paper, and turned away.

"Wait a minute, ma'am." The clerk was calling her back. Was she made?

Immy froze for a moment, then turned back toward him, slightly, still keeping her head down.

"Your change. You forgot your change."

Whew. Her secret was safe.

"OK," she said. Damn! She hadn't been going to say anything so they couldn't hear what her voice sounded like. "OK," she repeated in a low, hoarse tone.

"Are you all right, ma'am?" He lowered his head, trying to peer into her eyes. She wasn't going to show him what color they were, no matter how hard he tried. She nodded, took the change, then fled.

Nine

"Oh, shoot."

"What is it, Imogene?" Hortense tore her attention away from the blaring quiz show for a few seconds.

"This stupid book." Immy waved *Criminal Pursuits* at her mother. "This is a stupid, stupid book."

"Books can't be stupid. Authors and readers can be, but books cannot."

"OK, so it's me that's stupid then. I thought this book would tell me how to be a criminal. Instead it tells how to pursue them."

Hortense shook her head. She glanced at the screen and said "What is triangulation?" to Alex Trebec.

You think you're so smart because you worked in a library and have a vocabulary. Immy looked daggers at her mother, but the exasperating woman, propped with all the available pillows on the motel bed, had turned back to the show. Immy threw the book onto the plastic laminated desk and retreated to the bathroom to think.

"Don't slam the door," Hortense called.

Immy clicked it shut, then plopped onto the side of the tub and tried to think what to do next. Someone must have cleaned the bathroom recently. The smell of disinfectant stung her nostrils. She tore off a strip of toilet paper and wiped the drip from the tip of her nose.

What did criminals do when they were on the lam? Except she wasn't a criminal, but the law thought she was, and her mother, too. Maybe, just maybe, Hortense *was* one.

A protective feeling stole over Immy, sort of a maternal warmth, toward Hortense. For all her feelings of superiority—

and Immy didn't doubt her mother considered herself superior to her daughter—it seemed Hortense was defenseless in this particular situation. This occurrence was highly unusual. Hortense had no experience dodging the law and being on the run. Of course, Immy didn't either, but she thought she might be able to figure out how to survive under the radar, having gotten this far. Her mother would never be able to do that.

Their motel hideout in Cowtail seemed perfect. No one knew where they were, even what town they were in. No one would find them here. If Immy could avoid being spotted when she went out to get food, they could stay here indefinitely. That thought led to her thinking about buying food. Food took money. When they ran out of money, they would be in trouble. How to get more money? Immy wondered if she could learn how to rob banks or maybe All Sips stores. People did it all the time. It couldn't be that hard. She would need a better disguise, though. She swiped at her nose with a new wad of toilet paper.

"Imogene, come in here!" Mother sounded like she was alarmed at something.

She flew out of the bathroom, banging the door against the thin plaster wall. "What is it? What's wrong?"

Her mother pointed to the TV screen. "Look, it's Xenia Blossom."

Sure enough, a picture of the waitress who had quit over the bottom-pinching incident filled the screen.

"She was in a catastrophic collision," said Hortense.

Immy dropped her wad of toilet paper to the floor.

They listened to the news report, which said Xenia had been involved in a car-combine crash outside Saltlick.

"It appears Blossom's car, traveling at a high rate of speed, rear-ended the slow-moving combine, an older model John Deere. The passenger in Blossom's vehicle and the driver of the combine were not harmed. Our information says that the damage to the stricken vehicle is said to be minor."

The news moved on to the upcoming bond election.

"What was a combine doing on the road this time of year?" said Immy. "There's nothing to harvest this early in the spring."

"It's that Pinkley boy," said Hortense. "They gave his name just before you got here. He bought a used one to rent out. I talked to his mama in the grocery store about a week ago. He was taking it home from the secondhand John Deere dealer. I hope it's not damaged irreparably."

"They said the damage was minor. What did they say about Xenia?"

"She's in the hospital, unconscious. They interviewed Cathy for about three seconds. She said she was at the window at the front of the Kut and Kurl and saw Xenia rush out of the restaurant and hasten to her car where she accelerated toward the highway."

"She peeled out, you mean."

"That is precisely the way Cathy verbalized it. Her car squealed around the corner to get over to the highway, she said."

"Cathy was on TV? I'll bet she liked that."

"Imogene, the woman is unconscious."

"Cathy, too?"

Hortense's bosom heaved with her heavy sigh. "Xenia is unconscious. But why was she in the restaurant? Xenia, not Cathy. Did she think she had to be working today?"

"She quit, Mother. She quit the same day I did. I was telling the truth about that. So, no, probably not. Maybe she hadn't heard the news about Uncle Huey."

"Poor Hugh. He lost you and Xenia the same day. He was going to be shorthanded. How could you do that to him?"

Poor Hugh! What about poor Imogene?

"The only clue they seem to have," said Hortense, "is a footprint. It seems a portion of the sausage that protruded from Hugh's orifice retained an imprint of footwear."

"A footprint? What kind?"

"They showed it on the television screen. It looked like the imprint of a cowboy boot, with the shape of the ball of the foot and the narrow heel. There was some sort of squiggle at the edge of the heel."

"Well, that's not a good clue. Half of Saltlick wears cowboy boots. Let's think about this. Detectives make lists. Let's make a list."

"A list of what?"

"Um, suspects, I think."

Immy's mother brightened at that. "That is a decent idea, Imogene." She swung her feet over the side of the bed and leaned toward Immy eagerly, setting her round elbows on her rotund knees. "Yes. I did not kill Huey, we know that, so someone else did. Good thinking, Imogene. Let's cogitate to figure out who did actually kill him."

"OK." Immy drew columns on a piece of motel stationery and headed one Suspects. "Should I put you down because the cops think you're good for it?"

"I'm not a suspect to us, just to the police. Whom do we suspect?"

Immy shrugged. Her pen hovered over the first column. If she had colored pens she could put her mother down in one color and the other suspects in another. She looked at her mother. Her mother looked back at her.

"Someone wearing cowboy boots," said Hortense.

"I'll write 'male Population of Saltlick.' Oh, some females, too, right?" Immy's pen, however, remained still.

"Don't be mouthy, Imogene. We know that someone killed him. He wouldn't choke himself on frozen sausage," said Hortense.

"Frozen sausage. That's a clue. So someone had to know where to get the sausage. It had to be someone who worked at the restaurant."

"No, not of a necessity." Hortense shook her head slowly and tapped a chubby forefinger on her lower lip. "Hugh could have just procured the sausage from the walk-in prior to the time when the murderer arrived."

"Maybe the murder brought it with him."

Hortense stared at Immy. "The murderer did not bring frozen sausage with him. People don't carry frozen sausage around. It was a, what do they call it a weapon of?"

"A weapon of opportunity?" That had been in her *Compleat* book.

Immy thought she saw a glint of admiration in her mother's eye. "Yes, that's it exactly."

"Does this tell us who murdered Uncle Huey?" asked Immy.

"No, but it makes me hungry, talking about sausage. Where's the nearest pizza place? What is that toilet tissue doing on the carpet?"

HORTENSE FINISHED LICKING THE LAST of the mozzarella cheese from her fingers, wiped them delicately on one of the brown napkins that had come with the pizza and soda, and took up the TV remote.

"Back to our list?" asked Imogene. "I think I know who a good suspect is."

Her mother looked at Immy with genuine interest. "Pray tell."

"Xenia. I'm putting her down."

"I thought she quit Hugh's employ and left well before the crime was committed."

"She could have come back. In fact, if she did murder Uncle Huey, she might have left incriminating evidence behind. She might have been there today to get it. Anyway, I've seen her wear cowgirl boots. I need to interview her."

"It will, I surmise, be a difficult interrogation. She's unconscious in the hospital."

That was true. Even if she regained consciousness, she was in a sort of public place where Immy would be recognized if she tried to go there to grill her.

Her mother found a channel she wanted and set the remote beside her on the bed. Immy moved from the bed to the chair at the desk, where she had left her two reference books. It was becoming more and more clear to Immy that she needed good disguises. She turned to the index of her *Moron's Compleat* book.

"It's here," she crowed. "Disguises is listed as a topic."

Her mother picked up the remote, muted the television and frowned. "Imogene, for cryin' out loud. Disguises *are* listed."

"Mother, there is an entry called 'Disguises' in the index."

"Oh." Hortense put the volume back on.

The text was disappointing, however. It listed sunglasses and hats as good disguises. Immy thought she would need a little more than that. What about wigs? She turned to the *Criminal Pursuits* book.

"Wow, it's here, too." Her second book turned out to be much more helpful. It suggested a wig, large sunglasses, which would be good, moles or beauty marks, and a fat suit, which it said was optional. "Good thing it's optional," muttered Immy, "because I don't know what it is." She flipped the page and read on. Further suggestions were to use an accent, change posture, use high heels, if female, to change height, and stay in the shadows whenever possible. Immy thought high heels, if male, might work, too, to disguise gender. Aha, she had thought of something the hotshot author hadn't.

There was a costume shop in Wymee Falls, but she wasn't sure she could get there and back without being spotted. She had gotten the pizza in Cowtail, a block away, by walking there and back, but she would have to drive to the costume shop. If the cops were on the lookout for her van, or if they'd set up roadblocks, she was sunk. She wished she knew someone who could tell her if the police had her plate number on a lookout list.

She wanted to call the costume shop to see if they had what she wanted, but she was afraid the call would be traced. She would just have to visit the place. What choice did she have? She would wait until after dark, then sneak into Wymee Falls and hope the costume shop had her equipment and was still open.

Ten

It was about seven. Darkness wasn't complete yet, but the spring dusk was gathering when Immy inched open the door of the motel room and peeked out. A steady stream of traffic droned by on the highway out front, but no one left the hard road and drove to the back of Cowtail's Finest. Looking out for people, she cleared the area to her left, but when she looked to her right, she saw Baxter Killroy come out a nearby door and stroll toward her. Too late to duck back into the room. He had spied her.

"Imogene." He smiled. That lazy, sexy smile. "What in the hell are you doing here?"

"Sh!" She edged out and closed the door behind her. "No one knows I'm here."

"Yeah, I've seen the TV. The cops are looking for you and your mother."

He didn't look like he was going to turn her in. She needed to make sure, though. "Baxter, I'm desperate. I need a favor."

He stuck his hand on the wall beside her and leaned close. "Anything, babe. Shall we go inside?" He tilted his cowboy hat toward the door of her room.

"No, no I don't think so." Immy hadn't been sure her mother would approve of her driving into town and exposing herself to danger, so she had waited until Hortense fell asleep. Bringing Baxter in would be sure to awaken her. Then her trip might be much harder to make.

"Why not?" Baxter said.

"I think, I think it's better not to go in."

Baxter straightened up and stared at her. "You have someone in there?"

"Well...."

"Little Imogene has a guy in her room?" He looked shocked but amused.

OK, let him think that, but what a dolt. Couldn't he figure out she would have her mother with her? And, hey, she wasn't that little.

"Baxter, please don't tell anyone you saw me here. Can you do that for me?"

He took a moment to think. "If you don't tell anyone you saw me."

"Fine." Maybe he could be even more helpful. She thrust her list at him. "Could you possibly pick these things up for me at the costume shop?"

"I was headed into the city just now. I guess I could." He squinted at the piece of paper in the dying light. "You want a blond wig and sunglasses? Hats?"

"Big ones. Big sunglasses and big hats. Regular-sized wig."

He kept reading. "What's a fat suit?"

"If they don't have it, don't get it. See if they have beauty marks, though. I'd appreciate it so much."

He leaned toward her again. "How much?"

"Let's wait and see." She tried a vampy little smirk. If he still thought there was another guy in the room when he returned, she would figure out what to do next. Maybe she could tip him, and they'd be square.

"Let's not wait," said Baxter as he slipped one hand to the small of her back and pulled her in tight. Before Immy could squeal, his mouth was on hers, and sparks were flying. They flew from Baxter's lips to hers, through her veins, her muscles, reaching every part of her body. The kiss was intense but short. As suddenly as he had grabbed her, he released his hold and sauntered away.

She watched his cute little Wrangler-ed butt disappear into the door he'd come from, waited for her heartbeat and her breath to return to normal, then stole back into her room, grateful she didn't have to brave Wymee Falls until she had disguises.

Mother wasn't asleep after all. "Imogene, I don't think I can wear these pants another day," said Hortense, raising her voice over the television volume. The vermillion polyester was starting to take on a brownish cast.

"Well, now, do you have any other pants with you?" Immy tried to do the sarcastic one-eyebrow lift, but she suspected they both went up, as they usually did.

"Can you not creep back into our house surreptitiously and obtain some of my clothing under the cover of darkness?"

She didn't know if she could or not, but a good PI should be able to do a B and E on her own home. She could probably get back to Cowtail's Finest by the time Baxter returned with the goods.

THE B AND E DIDN'T TURN OUT to be all that easy. The plan was to park outside town and walk in. Saltlick was such a small town, the distance from the edge of it to their trailer wasn't far. Since it was almost eight and getting dark, if she were careful, no one would spot her.

There was a dirt lot at the edge of town where a big oil tanker, minus the cab, sat most of the time. Smaller tank trucks would cart oil in from local wells and dump it into the large one and, when it was full, a semi cab would hook up to it and take it to the refinery in Houston. She tucked the van behind the big tanker trailer and sussed out her surroundings.

The pump jack from a nearby oil well clanked and creaked. There were two wells in town, a small one and this huge one next to the lot. Immy strained to hear any other noises, but the pump was too noisy.

She slid from the car, wincing at the dome light when she pushed the door open. She wished she knew how to turn that bright beacon off, but she had no idea. That probably wasn't in either of her books. She was greeted by the familiar, slightly rancid smell of oil being brought to the surface of modern-day America after rotting deep in the recesses of history for eons. Dead dinosaurs, her mother had always told her, deceased prehistoric beasts. The smell didn't remind her of anything alive, that was for sure.

"Hi, Immy," called old Mrs. Jefferson.

Immy froze. Bent nearly double from osteoporosis, Mrs. Jefferson walked by with her ancient, waddling basset hound on a leash. Immy waved, knowing she would never hear an answer. The woman was deaf as a cactus. Immy waited until they shuffled out of sight, wiped the sweat from her forehead, and proceeded.

It was only four blocks from the lot to her house, but tonight, of course, it was a bustling four blocks. She could have sworn there were more people out tonight than she had ever seen at the Memorial Day Parade. She hadn't bothered with a disguise for this mission, counting on the dead of night to cover her tracks.

She had wisely, she thought, worn her flip-flops because they were black, but their *thwack, thwack, thwack* as she tried to steal through the night undetected cancelled the stealth factor of the color.

Chained in the side yard, the Wilson's ancient Rottweiler growled, then barked, as she tried to sneak by. He set off the pair of beagles next door, and they passed the relay baton off to Lacy, the cute little cocker spaniel in the next block. In every yard, people sitting sipping sweet tea or beer raised a hand in greeting.

Maybe they couldn't see who she was. After all, it could be that they were just being neighborly because someone was passing by, someone they'd never be able to ID in a lineup, she hoped.

The block before her house, all fell quiet. No one was about, and no dogs were chained in the yards. But the trailer she came to before hers harbored a vicious, dark Brahma hen named Larry Bird. She had been given the name when she was just a young chick, and a wrong gender had been determined. By the time she started laying eggs, the name had become stuck. The feisty fowl was usually in a somewhat flimsy pen behind the trailer, but it must have escaped tonight. That was not an unusual occurrence.

Larry Bird rushed at Immy's ankles without a warning cluck, nipped and drew blood. As chickens go, she was enormous, Brahmas being one of the larger breeds of fowl.

"Shoo, shoo," Immy whispered as urgently as she could without shouting. She flapped her hands at the menace, but Larry kept coming, ducking and darting, nipping one of Immy's ankles. Immy jumped onto the lowest branch of the magnolia tree in the neighbor's front yard and kicked down at her to make her go away, but Larry only bit at her flip-flop. Her leap had shaken one off. The chicken ran back in the direction of its pen with her flip-flop prize.

"You damn Larry Bird," she yelled, then cringed, hoping no one had heard her. She waited a few minutes, but the hen didn't return. Should she go after it and retrieve her footwear, or should she go to her home and get her sneakers?

She decided not to walk through chicken droppings with one bare foot—one bleeding bare foot. She jumped down and dashed safely to her own trailer.

Once inside, she sank onto the welcoming plaid couch. It didn't seem old and worn out in the darkness. It seemed heavenly and smelled like home. Her head fell back, and she closed her eyes. She mustn't fall asleep, though. She had to snatch some clothes and be back by the time Baxter returned to Cowtail from Wymee Falls with her disguises.

She tugged two suitcases out from under Hortense's bed, opened drawers in both bedrooms, and threw clothing into them for her and her mother, flinging aside items she didn't think they would need. She stuck a few things in for Drew, too. Not wanting anyone to know she was there, she left the lights off and worked in the dark.

It was hard finding a pair of shoes. She crawled around on the floor of her tiny closet, trying to match two of them. For the first time in her life, she wished she were like her mother, who lined her shoes up neatly every night instead of kicking them into the closet. Immy owned two more pairs of sneakers besides the ones she had with her at the motel, a worn-out pair she was saving in case she ever did yard work or perhaps painting, and a white pair she saved in case she wanted to go someplace special and have clean, white shoes. They were the same brand and style, one pair new and one old. Without light, however, she couldn't tell which was which, so she picked up both pairs, put two shoes on after pulling on a pair of socks, and tossed the other two into the suitcase. In the process, most of the closet floor got emptied out into the room.

Ready to exit, she remembered her phone charger. She usually kept it in a kitchen drawer but not a specific one. She opened the junk drawer and spread her palms atop the items, but she wasn't able to feel the charger. She pulled the contents out: hammer, screwdriver, pair of pliers, wine opener, and about forty dry ballpoint pens, piling the contents onto the counter. No phone charger. The next drawer was the knife drawer. Should she chance it? No, she would probably slice her fingers. Hortense kept phone directories in the next drawer. She was reluctant to throw old ones away for some reason Immy could never fathom. Immy heaped that drawer's contents on the counter, beginning to give up hope of finding her charger. The pens and the hammer clattered to the floor when she drew the phone books out and shoved them onto the countertop.

Then she came across a flashlight in the next drawer, which held mostly kitchen linens. By some miracle, it shone. Weakly, the batteries on their last ions, or whatever batteries use to produce current, but it gave light. The counter was now a mess. But there, plugged into the socket next to the microwave, was her charger. She clutched it, triumphant, and got ready to leave.

Once again, she put her ear to the front door and listened for passersby. She grabbed an umbrella from the stand next to the coat closet so she could fend off Larry Bird if she should attack again, but her return trip was mercifully uneventful.

WHEN BAXTER RETURNED FROM WYMEE FALLS, he banged on the flimsy motel room door so loudly he woke up Hortense.

She sat up on the bed and tucked the spread around her chins. "Don't answer it!"

Immy tiptoed to the door and peeked through the hole. "It's just Baxter, Mother."

"How does he know we're here?"

"I'll explain later." Baxter stuck his head into the room before he entered. "Mrs. Duckworthy." He strolled in and gave her the unsexy version of his smile. "I thought you were a guy."

Hortense beamed him her best evil eye. "Why would you think that?" Immy knew she was sensitive about her appearance. It may lack many things, Immy knew, but her looks would never lead a person to believe she wasn't a female.

"Well, Immy said …"

Immy's kick to his booted ankle shut him up. "Do you have the goods?" she said. "Were they still open?"

"Sure. They closed at eight. I was there in plenty of time." He handed her a shopping bag and, separately, the receipt. Immy dug the money out of her purse and added an extra two dollars. "For gas," she told him. The other shopping bag seemed to be full of cold remedies when she peeked into it, but Baxter didn't sound like he was sick. He looked confused when he left.

"Would you mind informing me of what is transpiring?"

Immy turned to give her mother an explanation. "I have a plan."

IMMY REMEMBERED, FROM VISITING HER father in the hospital as he lay dying from his gunshot wounds, that visiting hours started at ten a.m. She had been only twelve, but there wasn't anything about his death that she didn't remember vividly. Surely, the hospital still had the same visiting hours.

She set out from Cowtail at nine-thirty, wearing the wig, one of the three wide-brimmed straw hats Baxter had bought, huge round sunglasses, and three beauty marks on her left cheek. She had been relieved Baxter hadn't found a fat suit. It didn't sound like a fun item of apparel.

The ever-present, incessant west wind buffeted her between the motel door and her car, so she held tightly to the hat. The wind in these parts was either blowing or blowing hard. It was never not blowing.

The only parking spot left in the lot was in a corner on the top tier. She hoped the van wouldn't be too noticeable there. A lot of pickup trucks kept it company. She checked her beauty spots in the rearview mirror and tilted the hat forward to hide more of her face. She could only hope Xenia had regained consciousness after her wreck with the combine. Nothing new had been reported about the case this morning on television. The reporters had merely rehashed the same material they'd given out the day before. They had added an outside shot of the restaurant, though. Hortense had surprised Immy by crying when she saw it.

Immy put her hand on the door handle to exit the van. Her palms and the bottoms of her feet prickled. "All right," she told herself. "You're frightened. That doesn't mean you can't do this." She smeared a little more of Hortense's bright red lipstick on her lips and opened the car door.

Her hat blew off. The wind whipped at the door. She tugged at the door handle, holding it against the rooftop gale so the hinges wouldn't break. After she clambered out and pushed the door shut, she watched her new hat sail over the parapet and dive toward the street below. It skidded toward the fountain by the front door, then disappeared around the other side of the hospital, rolling on its brim. She held tightly to her wig and hurried to the elevator.

The front desk jockey wouldn't tell her what room Xenia was in unless she was a relative.

"I'm her cousin. Her cousin Millie."

The receptionist didn't look as if she believed her, but she didn't challenge her statement either. "Ms. Blossom has a visitor with her. When he leaves you can go up."

"Who is it? Cousin Ned?"

"I believe it's her husband."

Immy sat on a hard vinyl chair and thought about that, frowning. A husband would be just as fictional as a Cousin Ned or a Cousin Millie. Xenia wasn't married, but she had been living with Frankie Laramie for a while. He had probably told the receptionist he was her husband so he could get up to the floor to see her. Frankie Laramie and Xenia Blossom were well matched, in Immy's opinion. Both were good looking but with an underlying crudeness about them. Xenia was most always dressed to play up her bosom. Frank, all spiked black hair and narrow pants, looked like some slick, big city gangster. He was a huge fan of Xenia's bosom, but he seemed to like Immy's, too. Immy was always a little uncomfortable around him. He had an uncle or cousin or something who owned the Wymee Falls franchise for The Tomato Garden restaurant. Frankie's sleazy-looking relative had started coming to Hugh's restaurant a few months ago. Hugh and the relative would go into the upstairs office and close the door to talk. Something was going on, but Immy wasn't sure exactly what.

When Frank stepped off the elevator and walked through the lobby, his head down and his steps dragging, Immy gave a shudder. He moved like a slow snake today. He looked up and saw her.

"Hi, Imogene," he said. She had never seen him look so bad. His dark eyes were underscored by matching hollows, and his clothes looked like he'd worn them for a few days. Frank was usually outfitted and pressed neat as a trussed turkey.

"I'm here incognito, Frankie." Damn, he'd seen right through her disguise.

He ignored her comment and dropped onto the chair next to hers. "She's bad off, Imogene." His voice cracked when he talked.

"Is she still unconscious?"

He balled one fist inside the other and twisted it against his palm. "I don't know if she's going to make it." Then he slowly turned to face her. "It's your family, that damn Hugh Duckworthy. It's his fault. He's your uncle." His knuckles turned white.

Immy drew back. He was blaming her for Xenia's accident? "I wasn't there, Frankie."

"But that damn Hugh was. She came storming out, said he refused to give her the last paycheck. She was madder'n a mad cow. Tore off and lost control of the car. Only reason I'm OK is because I had my seatbelt on. She didn't. She got tossed out of the convertible and she looked ..." He gulped loudly, and his eyes misted. "She looked so broken."

"Xenia fought with Hugh right before her wreck yesterday?"

"That's what I said, didn't I?"

"Yesterday?" She couldn't have fought with Hugh. He'd died three days before that. Why had Xenia lied to Frank?

"Have you seen a newspaper lately?" she asked him.

He looked at Immy like she was a two-headed goat. "I don't read newspapers."

Of course not. "Have you seen any TV this week?"

"Just Xenia's soaps." He got his pack of Virginia Slims out of his shirt pocket and fingered the wrapper.

So, maybe he still didn't know Hugh was dead. She bet he didn't know she and Hortense were wanted either. That was a relief anyway. He wouldn't be likely to rat them out.

"I'm glad now that damn Hugh never hired me."

"I didn't know you applied for work at the restaurant."

"Yeah, but he wouldn't take me on."

"Can't you work in your own family's restaurant? Don't some of the Laramies own The Tomato Garden in Wymee Falls?"

"It's a franchise, and my Uncle Guido has it. He's not exactly a Laramie. He's a Giovanni, Ma's brother. No way I'd work for him, though. He's a slave driver." Meaning, Immy thought, Frank would like a job but wouldn't actually like to work. He hadn't had Hortense for a mother.

"Is that who I used to see talking to Hugh up in his office, your Uncle Guido?"

"You know the interstate loop they keep talking about?" Immy nodded. "It's supposed to go awful close to Huey's Hash. Guido thought that would be a good location for another Tomato Garden. He's been trying to get Hugh to sell it to him."

Should she tell Frank? *Oh, go ahead. It might be interesting to see his reaction.*

"Frankie, Hugh was dead when Xenia got in her wreck. He was found dead the day before that, probably killed even earlier, the day before that."

"Huh? She sounded hysterical when she ran out of there. Wasn't making a whole lot of sense. I thought she said she was pissed at Hugh, but maybe it was someone else she was mad at. Who else would have been there?"

"Clem?"

Frank glanced at his Timex. "I gotta get going. I need to go to the unemployment office and fill out my monthly paperwork." *The ideal job for Frankie, money and no work. And you need a smoke,* thought Immy.

He shambled out through the revolving door, and Immy hightailed it up to Xenia's room. Maybe Xenia would wake up.

SHE DIDN'T, AND IMMY LEFT after watching Xenia breathe for about ten minutes. She looked like a nicer person when she wasn't awake, but maybe most people do, thought Immy. Her bleached blonde hair fanned out on the white pillowcase, below the bandages framing her pale face. She looked especially washed out without her usual cotton candy pink lipstick. Her breasts, two huge mounds under the thin sheet, rose and fell, so Immy knew she was alive.

Also, the machines pulsed and beeped with what they called on TV her vital signs, but Immy didn't know which one was for her brain, if any of them were. If Xenia's brain was dead, and she had killed Uncle Huey, it might never be known for sure who bumped him off.

Immy made her way out of the hospital slowly, hanging onto her wig when she got outside and trying to put some possibilities together in her mind. Maybe Frank had been trying to throw Immy off by telling her Xenia saw Hugh after he was dead. Maybe Frank killed Uncle Huey. Would she know if he was lying to her? She would have to see if there was a chapter in either of her books about how to tell when people were lying.

She tried to imagine how this scenario might have come about. Frank doted on Xenia, and Hugh fired Xenia. Would Frank be angry enough to kill Hugh? It didn't seem like it, but maybe Frank's hot temper got the better of him. His mother's family was Italian, after all, Giovannis from El Paso. Everyone knew Italians were hot blooded.

Her head was down, pondering how to determine Frank's guilt or innocence, as she entered the bottom floor of the dark, cool parking garage, glad to be out of the wind. The smell of cigarette smoke made her stop and fan the air in front of her. Then she heard the whispers.

"What the hell you think? I told you a million times, I'm-a retired."

Where were the whispers coming from?

"Just one more, Uncle Guido. You used to do this in Naples. I know you could do it." That was Frankie Laramie's voice. He had raised his volume on the last sentence. But where were they?

"Shush! You don't want nobody to hear this, do you? Of course I could-a do it, but do I wanna, that's the question."

"I know he's responsible for Xenia's wreck. I just know it." Frank was whispering again. "He should pay. It's for family, Uncle Guido."

"Stop sayin' my name, *cretino*. If I do whack-a him, it'll be the last job ever for me. *Capisce?* And you'll owe me somethin', family or no."

Immy heard footsteps coming toward her and looked around, frantic. A large trash barrel stood out about a foot and a half from the concrete wall. She squeezed in behind it, hoping the dim lighting would help conceal the parts of her that were going to stick out.

The footsteps stopped, however, before they reached her hiding place. Two car doors clicked open and slammed closed, then two separate engines started up. She stood abruptly, thinking it might look bad if she were seen hiding. Also, she wanted to see the cars.

The trash barrel went over with a clang that echoed up the ramp down which Frank's noisy vehicle was coming. He was proud of his glass mufflers that shook the whole car. He liked to sit and rev the stupid thing outside the diner. Immy ducked into the stairwell and dashed up the stairs as fast as a jackrabbit. She knew what Guido's car looked like. The two were definitely Frankie and Guido, and she didn't want Guido to see her.

She sat in her car for a full five minutes while her breathing returned to normal. It had sounded like Frank's Uncle Guido was going to kill someone. Isn't that what whack meant? But they must not have seen her, since no hit man came for her. Her hands still shook, though, as she buckled her belt and started down the hospital parking ramp.

That word, whack, kept bouncing around in her brain, stopping all other thoughts. It was a scary word. Maybe being a PI was too frightening.

She was careful to drive the speed limit. It wouldn't do to get nabbed for a traffic violation when she was a wanted woman and in disguise. She hightailed it toward her hideout to add

Frank's name to her list of suspects. Well, not hightailed exactly, since she did go the speed limit, more like slowtailed it. But, before she left Wymee Falls, an office supply store caught her eye. She thought it would be a good idea to color code the suspects on her list, and she needed supplies for that. Since she was still wearing most of her disguise, now would be a good time to shop for them.

Lamenting the loss of the floppy-brimmed hat, she held tightly to her wig as she got out of the car. The wind hadn't died down any. It howled around the corner of the brick building and cut off when she got inside. Immy took a deep breath. An office supply store had a certain comforting, happy smell. Maybe it was all the paper. She always loved coming here.

Momentarily forgetting the amount of money she had left, she filled a basket with pens, pencils, notepads, Post-its, a stapler, a hole punch, a nice sharp letter opener, a cork board, and multicolored push pins. She arrayed her items on the checkout counter, her heart lifting at the sight of all those lovely office supplies.

The bored male cashier rang them up. "That'll be sixty-four ninety-five."

She got out her wallet. Oops. "I think I'll have to put some back."

"Ma'am, you have something on your face."

Immy touched her cheek and came away with a beauty mark stuck to her forefinger. She gritted her teeth, shoved a couple items toward the insolent twerp, slapped down her money, and scooted out of the store.

As she drove away, she pulled her bag into her lap to inventory her purchase. She had ended up with a set of colored pencils, the push pins, and the letter opener.

A check in the rearview mirror revealed one beauty mark still pasted to her cheek. She ripped it off and flung it out the window.

The movement caused her wig to come halfway off. Disgusted with the whole ineffectual disguise thing, she decided to jettison it, too. Unfortunately, the wig was tangled in the handle of the plastic bag that held her newly purchased treasures, so they went out the window with it.

Slamming on the brakes, she pulled to the roadside shoulder, intending to retrieve her pencils and pins. She needed the pencils to color-code her list. A dark SUV that seemed to have been traveling at a high rate of speed squealed its tires as it swerved around her. A loud report sounded.

At first Immy thought a gun had been fired, and she ducked low behind the steering wheel. Then she saw the car, now in front of her, sag to the right. Was that her letter opener sticking out of the flattened tire?

Sirens wailed behind her, coming closer.

Had the rude clerk fingered her? Was she made? Were the cops onto her? She pulled out onto the road and sped away. The sirens continued screaming, wailing, up and down, drilling into her brain.

She kept her grip on the steering wheel, but sweat oozed from her palms, sprang to her forehead, and dripped beneath her arms. She had never been in a high-speed chase before.

As she reached the edge of Wymee Falls, the sirens came to an abrupt stop. She chanced a glance in the rearview mirror. They were stopping at the SUV with the flat tire.

Close call. They weren't going to nab her, at least not today.

But her hands didn't stop shaking until she had been back in the motel room for at least an hour.

Eleven

Detective Immy needed more information. She needed to inspect the scene of the crime further. If Clem could go inside the diner when it was roped off with police tape, so could she. Maybe the tape was gone by now anyway. How long did they leave that stuff up?

She didn't expect the diner to be open for business, but it was. What was Clem thinking of? It had to be him that opened it up. That just didn't seem decent to Immy.

Five white pickups were nosed into the curb in front of Huey's Hash, and as she walked past, again in disguise, two leather-skinned ranchers came out the front door rubbing their bellies and smiling. They looked vaguely familiar, and one nodded to her. They were probably semi-regular customers. They wouldn't know her in disguise, so they were no doubt just being polite. Clem might see through it, though. She had better not go in.

Immy returned to the alley where she had stealthily parked the van and decided she would have to come back when the restaurant was closed. She picked up a bucket of chicken for her mother and her for lunch at the drive-through chicken place in Cowtail, then hunkered down at the hideout until nighttime when she could use the cover of darkness.

A good operative knew when to carry out covert missions, or was she straying from private eye into thriller territory with that thought?

You never knew how spooky a place was until you tried to sneak around in it at night. She waited until midnight, a time when most Saltlickians were in bed. The van sounded like a motorcycle roaring through the quiet, deserted streets. She passed close enough to the police station to see that both official cars were parked there. As far as she could tell, she wasn't detected hiding the van in the back of the diner again, where Clem usually parked.

She still hadn't figured out how to turn off the dome light, and she let out a squeak when it lit up the alley as she opened the van door. Then she let out a louder squeak when the sound of the door slamming reverberated off the solid back wall of the eatery like a rifle shot. This definitely felt much more like a thriller than a detective story lately. She hadn't read many thrillers, but she hoped they had happy endings.

It was hard to tell if anyone had heard her. She doubted she could have heard a siren over the pounding she felt in her ears. Was her heart going to explode? After five full minutes of standing stock still and no one appearing, she approached the back door, her heart pounding slightly slower. A dog barked in the distance, a disinterested bark like his heart wasn't in it. Some early crickets, stirred by the warmer weather, sang somewhere nearby.

She tried the back door to the diner. It was locked. She was not going to return to the motel and tell her mother she had failed in her reconnaissance. Hortense had actually condoned the idea and said it was a good thing Immy had thought of it. Immy knew better than Chief Emmett and Officer Ralph what belonged in the diner and what didn't. If the killer left evidence, it made eminent sense, according to Hortense, that Immy could suss it out. "Suss it out" was Immy's phrase, not her mother's. "Scrutinize with a greater degree of success than the authorities" was Mother's terminology.

A memory came back to her in a flash. On a normal day, Clem was always there before Uncle Huey and usually the first one in the place, but one day Hortense had dropped Immy at work because it was raining too hard to walk. The front door had been locked, so Immy had dashed around to the back, lamenting the van's departing tail lights. She had seen Clem unlocking the back door.

Before he saw her, he had reached up and stowed the key above the door jamb. Maybe it was still there. Immy tried to feel for the key above the door, but she couldn't quite reach the place. Clem was taller than she was. The big green dumpster container stood beside the door. If she could get on top of that, she should be able to reach the key, if it was still there.

She eyed the dumpster. How to get up on it? She opened the passenger door of the van, stood on the seat, and reached up for the lid of the dumpster. Maybe if she jumped. The third try worked, and she landed on the lid. If only that dome light in the van would burn out. She stuck her foot out and kicked the door closed to turn the light off. Then it took her a few moments to adjust her eyes to the dark alley. She was going to ignore the small animal sounds coming from behind the bin. She would assume the rats were busy on their own business errands and wouldn't bother her.

Damn. The dumpster was farther from the diner door than she thought. If only she had pushed it over before she got on top of it. She would have to lean way over to reach the top of the door.

She clung to the side jamb of the door with one hand, stretched, and felt along the crumbling wood at the top with the other. Dust showered down. Immy controlled a shudder so she wouldn't fall off the trash bin. Was it her imagination, or was she dislodging dead insects—or worse, live ones? Spiders? Tarantulas? Maybe scorpions?

There, metal! She had found the key. She curled her fingers around it and carefully straightened up, bringing her center of gravity back to the top of the bin. Her smile seemed to split the darkness, and a tiny giggle escaped.

Looking up to thank the heavens, she closed her eyes and took a step back.

Only half of the dumpster lid was in place, the half she stood on. The other half stood propped open. The yawning chasm below looked empty in the dark as she fell, but as Immy landed in it, she could tell it was nearly full. Of garbage, of course. Rotting lettuce, tomatoes, meat, paper plates smeared with BBQ sauce and French fry grease, coffee grounds, and a lot of other things reeking of former food stuffs she couldn't identify. And rats. There may have been some in the alley, but there were definitely lots of them in the bin. She told herself she was not going to throw up.

The only good thing about the great quantity of garbage was that the high level made it easy for Immy to climb out. She threw a leg over the top of the bin, hung from the edge, and dropped to the ground.

She shook potato peelings from her hair, swallowing the bile swimming toward the top of her throat, and swiped at the disgusting bits of foul-smelling refuse clinging to her clothing. She doubled, then tripled her determination not to throw up.

It worked. Despite the way she knew she looked and smelled, she felt good. She had the key. She could carry out her mission.

After she unlocked the back door, she crept through the hallway and into the kitchen. Why hadn't she brought a flashlight? On TV the crime scene inspectors always had flashlights. She didn't dare turn on any overhead lights. Emmett and Ralph did occasionally patrol the streets of Saltlick.

Think, Immy, think. What would a detective do at a dark scene?

Probably bring a flashlight. But a brainstorm occurred to her. She felt proud to think of cracking open the refrigerator door an inch. That hadn't been in her book, but it should have been. She would have to write to the editor. Maybe she should write her own book.

The dim bulb did a surprisingly good job of illuminating the kitchen. She examined the floor, looking for any evidence of the exact place Uncle Huey had died, not wanting to step there. She couldn't tell where it had been, though. Whoever cleaned it up had done a good job.

In fact, the kitchen didn't look any different than usual. Nothing was out of place. Immy shrugged. It stood to reason there wouldn't be any evidence here. Being open for business today would have destroyed it. She had almost forgotten about that.

Maybe there would be some clues remaining in Hugh's upstairs office. She mounted the stairs noiselessly.

The shade was pulled down in the one window over Hugh's desk, but the streetlamp outside gave her more than adequate light when she reeled the shade up a foot. She was able to read the papers on his desk, but they were all order forms for supplies and groceries. There was nothing that indicated he was afraid or that his life was in danger, nothing that said, "If you find me dead, X is responsible."

Immy started to panic, thinking she wouldn't find any clues. Her whole ordeal was going to be wasted.

The desk drawers held old-fashioned ledgers, but Immy suspected they were from the days when her grandparents ran the restaurant. Hugh kept his records on his computer, and that was gone, probably confiscated as evidence.

Discouraged and stinking like a landfill, she slunk down the stairs. Hugh's parsley plant caught her eye, drooping in the window of the dining room. She had watered it her last day there, but that was four days ago. The poor thing needed water at least every other day. She stuck a finger in it to check the soil. Yep, it was dry, but her finger ran into something else buried in the dirt.

A cigarette butt. She pulled it out and examined it. If she squinted in the dim light, she could make out the logo on the filter: Virginia Slims. She didn't know anyone but Frankie Laramie who smoked Virginia Slims.

A clue? Had she found a clue? She bounced up and down a couple of times on the balls of her feet. She would be a detective yet. She stuck the butt back in the dirt but left it sticking out so it could be found. She didn't want to destroy the evidence she had found.

Now she needed to remain calm and cool. And casual. It was important she do this just right. Her whole body vibrated. She picked up the kitchen phone using a dishtowel so she wouldn't get fingerprints on it and dialed 9-1-1.

When the operator asked her to state her emergency, she flipped the corner of the towel over the mouthpiece to disguise her voice. She was coming up with all sorts of clever ideas.

"Important evidence at Huey's Hash. Overlooked by police. Clue in parsley pot. Check out Frankie Laramie."

She had done it! The police had all the evidence they needed to nab the perp. She dropped the phone in her excitement, then put it back in its cradle. Picked it up again and wiped off the prints she had just put on it.

Then she danced out the door, locked it, and sped back to the motel before she could be nabbed red-handed at the scene of the crime.

As soon as she walked into the motel room, Immy locked herself in the bathroom, stripped off her disgusting clothes, and stood under the stream of hot, clean water, grateful she had been able to secure more clothing the night before. She toweled off and, lacking pajamas which she had unfortunately forgotten all about, put on lovely, fresh garments: clean underwear, jeans, and t-shirt.

She came out of the bathroom to get her shoes on. Then she remembered she hadn't gotten any extra socks. Damn.

Feeling suddenly weary and sodden, she sat on the edge of the cot to pull on the same pair she had been wearing for days now. The left one had spots of blood from the places Larry Bird had pecked her ankle. It had bled off and on all day. She lay back and held her foot up. Did it look infected?

Before she could worry any more about it, she heard Mother's voice. Immy had fallen asleep on the cot with a filthy sock in her hand.

"Are you going out to get breakfast?" asked Mother.

Immy rubbed her eyes. That had been a short night. "Maybe we could wait a while and get brunch."

Hortense's face fell. Did she look thinner today? Immy knew her mother could stand to miss a few meals, although she never did, but they were both under so much stress now, running from the law, Hortense was probably even hungrier than usual.

Immy felt sorry for her and gave in to her sad eyes. "I'll go get something, Mother."

"Please be very careful, dear. Take extra precautions. If you should be apprehended, I don't know what I'd do."

Immy also didn't know what she would do, what either one of them would do. There was no use thinking about it. She must not get caught. That's all there was to it.

Hortense watched Immy count the bills she had left. "We can't afford to keep getting take-out food," she said. "Maybe you could pick up a hot plate and something we can cook here in the room."

"Hey, that's a great idea."

Hortense beamed, the first smile Immy had seen from her since they became desperadoes.

"I'll get some soup and some canned ravioli, maybe some SpaghettiOs."

Hortense sighed with a dreamy look. She loved SpaghettiOs. "That would be quite lovely."

Immy regretted the rash impulse that had compelled her to jettison the wig inadvertently, but she still had two more hats and the oversized sunglasses. She tucked her clean, straight hair up under the blue hat and set the sunglasses on her nose. She thought she could chance the All Sips in the neighboring small town of Range City for the supplies. She didn't go there often and hadn't been there in disguise at all. It was full daylight, though. If she saw any people she knew she would have to try to avoid them.

"Wait, dear," said Hortense. "Isn't that Xenia's boyfriend?"

Immy stared at the television screen where Hortense was pointing. Frank Laramie was being led into the Saltlick police station in handcuffs. "Turn it up," Immy said, perching next to her mother on the bed.

"… in connection with the recent bizarre slaying in this quiet town. The anonymous informant has not been identified to us, but the authorities have told us they are certain of his identity."

"How did the Wymee Falls station get a camera person to Saltlick in time to film Francis Laramie being taken into custody?" said Hortense.

No one but Mother would ever call Frankie Laramie Francis. He probably hated that name, too. Who wouldn't? "How do they know who the caller is?" said Immy. "I don't think they know his identity. It's not a him."

Hortense turned from the screen and gave Immy a speculative look. "And how do you know that?"

"I'll be back as soon as I can, Mother." Immy jumped up and left the room.

When she drove around the motel building and onto the hard top, she saw that Baxter's pickup was gone. Maybe he had moved out. Why on earth had he been staying in the motel to begin with? He lived in Saltlick, and it was close, only one town over. Had he come here to meet a woman at Cowtail's Finest? A similar establishment was where Nancy Drew Duckworthy had gotten her start, so Immy knew about places like this. A streak of rebellious adolescence, too many longnecks, and a dark-eyed, smooth-talking truck driver had been Immy's downfall. If only some men didn't have such dark eyes and talk so silky.

After she found out she was pregnant, she had tried to track down the truck driver. This was well before she had serious ideas about being a private eye, and she had neglected to get his name. She never saw him again. Immy's pregnancy had taken a lot of the starch out of Hortense, as well, but, after the adorable baby was born, Hortense fell in love with her granddaughter and never said another word about Immy's egregious lapse, as she had been terming her daughter's ill-advised behavior until then.

Immy knew she was lucky Hortense had continued to support her and hadn't kicked her out of the house to fend for herself. Two of Immy's high school classmates had gotten pregnant much too young and much too unmarried, and their parents had turned their backs on them. They had it rough, still did.

After Hortense's retirement, her pension from the library supported the three of them adequately enough for their basic needs. Imogene had taken whatever jobs she could until she graduated from high school, and Uncle Huey hired her as a waitress. After a few years of that, though, Immy began to picture herself working there forever, growing old, shuffling and still waiting on tables. Bringing people their orders with a shaky hand, mixing the orders up, and making zero tips for being such a bad waitress. What would her dear, departed, sainted father think of her, working a dead-end job her whole life? Not that she would ever phrase her question that way to her mother.

It was about time to hang a shingle and solve cases, to be a PI.

She got a library card before she could read, since her mother was a librarian. As soon as she could read, she started through the mysteries and thrillers in the crumbling little local library where Hortense worked. When they were exhausted, she wrangled a card from the much bigger Wymee Falls institution and was now about two-thirds finished with the mysteries that graced the metal shelves in those cool, lofty rooms. That had been the extent of her preparation for her life's work of detecting until she found the *Compleat Guide*.

The shopping trip was uneventful. No beauty spots came unglued, her hat didn't blow off, and her glasses, though they made it difficult to read the labels when she was inside the store, enabled her to see well enough to buy her supplies and get back to Cowtail's Finest. Maybe she was getting the hang of the disguise thing.

Immy drove around to the back of the motel and carted in her purchases. Baxter's truck was back, so he hadn't moved out. She would have to find out what he was doing here.

Hortense acted like it was Christmas, and she was unwrapping gifts.

"Oh, look, Cheetos!" She clapped her hands. "Goody, you got the hotplate, and how about this? Crunchy peanut butter!"

"Well, I figured we could have crunchy since Drew isn't here." Drew ate only creamy.

Hortense paused, a can of beef stew in each hand. "Do you think we should check on her?"

"I called Clem from the car. He said she's doing fine. He took her to daycare." Immy made a mental note to call again tonight, though. She would like to talk to Drew in person and make sure she was all right, not that she didn't trust Clem. "Tomorrow's Saturday. Maybe he can bring her somewhere, and we can have lunch together."

A dopey expression stole over Hortense's broad face. "Clem's a sweetheart, isn't he?"

Immy wouldn't exactly call him a sweetheart. His temper in the kitchen was legendary, but fiery explosions seemed to be the norm for cooks, from what waitresses who had worked at other places told her. She was sure he'd take good care of Drew, though. She had tried to warn him about Frankie's Uncle Guido over the phone. What if Clem was the target? Did he understand the implications?

"Clem, you should be careful for a while," she had said.

"Why is that?"

"There may be a contract out on you."

"I Iuh?"

"Did you talk to Xenia just before her accident?"

"Nope, didn't see her that day," he'd said.

Immy hadn't seen any grilling techniques to use over the phone in her *Compleat Guidebook*, so she had dropped the subject. Maybe someone else had upset Xenia, but who? Hugh had been dead, and Clem said he hadn't seen her. Who would have been at the diner but Clem?

"Has there been any more news about Frankie or the murder?" Immy asked Hortense, setting the last can on the desk to make a mini-pyramid.

"It seems he was interrogated and released."

"Released? Why would he be released?" Immy crumpled the empty plastic bags and stuffed them into the wastebasket.

"Perhaps because he didn't commit the crime?"

"But what about the cigarette butt?"

"What cigarette butt?"

Pounding shook the door, and both women jumped.

"What should we do, Imogene?" Hortense whispered.

Immy whispered back. "We should see who's at the door."

For some reason, Hortense squatted behind the bed, emitting a loud "Oof!" as she fell off her haunches and her rear end slammed onto the thin carpeting.

Immy peered out the peephole but couldn't see anyone. She made sure the chain was on and cracked the door open.

"Hey, babe." Baxter stood to the side of the door and tilted his head to see through the narrow opening. "Let me in."

Immy unhooked the chain, and Baxter slipped in. "Where's your Ma?"

"She's, um …"

Her mother's voice came from the floor behind the bed. "Imogene, assist me, please."

It took both of them to haul Hortense to her feet. She smoothed her checked pants and sat on the bed with as much dignity as she could muster. "I'm grateful to you for your timely assistance, Baxter."

"You're welcome, ma'am."

Was that a smirk on his face? Immy gave him a glare. People did not smirk at her mother. "What do you want, Baxter?"

"Hey, what's the matter?"

"That's what I'm asking you."

The television, its volume low, droned through a soap opera in the background. He swiped his hat off his head and rumpled his glossy curls. "I was wondering if you could do me a favor, Immy."

She waited to hear what the favor was before she agreed.

"I did you one," he said.

That was true, but she had tipped him two dollars. "I'm not going to agree until you tell me what you want me to do."

He frowned.

"What? That's only reasonable."

"You're in no position to make demands, you know. The police are looking for you."

"Are you threatening me?"

Those lazy, hooded eyes got shifty looking. "Maybe."

Immy's mind worked furiously. Would Baxter go to the police? Ever since she had known him, which was a couple of years now, he'd avoided the cops. When Chief Emersen or his officer ate at the restaurant, he'd be so busy taking out trash or mopping the floors that he couldn't bus any dining room tables until they left. She exchanged a look with her mother. Hortense gave her head a slight shake. No, she didn't think he would follow through, either.

"What is it you want?"

"It's not much, Immy." He bestowed his sexy smile on her. "I don't want anyone to know I'm here. Just like you. So, you don't tell, and I won't tell. Deal?"

"That sounds fine." What was the big deal about that? That was understood to be honor among thieves or whatever kind of criminals they both were. She ushered him out. After she closed the door she wondered if she had blown the chance to find out what he was doing at the motel in the first place. There wasn't an APB out on him that she knew of.

"Imogene, that man will not go to the authorities. He has an aversion to law enforcement, you know." Hortense made herself comfortable, plumping the pillows and settling back among them. She clicked the remote to change the channel and raise the volume.

"I do know, but I don't know why," said Immy.

"He was incarcerated," said Hortense.

"He did hard time? I knew it. When? What for?"

"He was imprisoned for making and selling methamphetamines."

"Wow, a meth head."

"I don't believe he partakes. I believe he only markets and manufactures it. That is, he used to. I doubt he does it anymore. I received the information from Hugh when he hired the man. Hugh actually consulted me about it, having his doubts as to whether or not Baxter Killroy could be trusted. He did not heed my advice, however, and decided to employ him anyway."

Immy's lips started tingling as her mind stubbornly returned to the steamy kiss he'd bestowed on her. She swiped her hand across her mouth to rub it away. She didn't want any more favors from Baxter.

"So he won't rat us out, but I wonder what he's doing here."

"That is not our problem. Would you mind warming some of that beef stew on the hot plate? My abdomen is communicating with me."

"What?" Sometimes her mother's convoluted language defeated her, even though she was used to it. "Oh, your stomach's growling?"

"That's what I said."

Immy was proud that she had remembered to buy a can opener. She opened the can and set it on the little burner her mother had placed on the flimsy veneer end table that sat between the double bed and the back wall.

After they ate their warmed, canned stew lunch, using plastic spoons and waxed paper bowls, Immy announced she had another plan.

"Maybe you should desist from making those plans, dear."

"Don't complain, Mother. I got you out of stir, didn't I?"

Hortense groaned. "Your language, dear."

"We need more information. We need to know why Frankie isn't being held and what the police know. Especially, we need to know if they know who the informant is. I'll be back soon."

Immy regarded her face in the bathroom mirror. Her fingers strayed to her lips. They didn't look different, but they still tingled a little. Baxter's kiss hadn't been half bad, she decided. Maybe she would brave another one. One kiss, that's all.

When she returned from her errand, she tried to high-five her mother, but Hortense refused.

"Baxter said I could borrow his truck, Mother."

"I am not able to invest any confidence in the words of Baxter Killroy, and you shouldn't either, little missy."

Not the little missy again. I hate that. Why does everyone think I'm so small anyway? But I will show her. It'll be OK.

Immy once again put on the beauty spots, only two this time, the sunglasses, and the hat she hadn't used yet. This one was almost a sombrero, the brim was so wide. The wind had picked up, and the air blew chill, so she also used the oversized sweater she had found in the van.

She drove Baxter's truck to the Saltlick police station and sat outside waiting for Ralph to emerge for lunch. She knew he almost always took his lunch after the chief. Ralph had invited her to dine with him many times, but she had always turned him down. She hoped he still wanted to.

Right on schedule at one-thirty sharp, he walked out of the door and over to the old Saltlick cop car, the one he always drove.

Immy cranked the window down. "Psst!"

Ralph's hand moved toward his pistol. He frowned at her. "Who are you? What are you doing in Killroy's truck?"

Shit, he knows the truck. "It's me, Immy."

Ralph squinted and took a step toward her. "What the hell?"

"I'm incognito."

He frowned harder.

"I'm in disguise. I'm wanted, aren't I?"

"Not really. That reporter must have gotten carried away," he said. "Chief doesn't think you or Hortense killed Hugh."

"Can you get in so we can go to lunch in Range City?"

Ralph grinned. "You want to go to lunch with me?" He poked a thumb at his broad chest. "You bet." He climbed into the passenger seat. There seemed to be less air with him in the truck, and there was certainly less room.

"We have to go to Sonic," Immy said, "so I don't get made."

"Immy, you won't get laid just going to lunch with me."

"Made, Ralph, made. I don't want to be recognized, and you don't want me to either. You shouldn't be associating with a felon."

"You're not a felon, Immy."

"Better safe than sorry. There's always a possibility of trumped-up charges, you know."

Immy headed toward Range City via the back roads. If Ralph knew Baxter's truck, probably everyone in Saltlick did. Immy never paid attention to people's vehicles, but some people apparently did. Now that she was acting as a PI, maybe she should start observing more details, like vehicles. Maybe even license plate numbers. She drove in silence for a few miles, wondering how to start. Unable to formulate a strategy, she shrugged and dived in.

"So," she said, starting her grilling, "what do you and Emmett know about the murder?"

At first she thought he wouldn't spill. He looked away from her, out the window, but then started to sing. "Not much. At least Chief hasn't told me much. He did say not to bother to bring you in, though."

"Huh? Why did he say that, because I'm not technically a felon?"

"I think Xenia Blossom is the new suspect."

Immy swerved but got back into her lane before hitting the oncoming truck. It honked long and loud anyway. Some drivers were so picky. "How can Xenia be a suspect? Did she wake up?"

"Naw. We got another anomalous tip."

"Anonymous, Ralph."

"That's what I said. Chief and me found some stuff in her purse."

Immy approached the outskirts of Range City and drove past the combination coin launderette/movie rental store.

"Incriminating evidence?" What kind of stuff would implicate Xenia in Huey's murder? A package of sausage? A pack of Virginia Slims? Some butts that matched the butt in the pot? Immy had never seen Xenia smoke, though. Maybe she carried Frankie's cigarettes for him.

"Yep."

"So, did the chief definitely say we're not wanted any more, Ralph, or are you supposed to maybe bring us in later?"

"Gosh, I'm not sure. He just said not to bring you in. He said, let's see, he said not to bother. Maybe if it's not a bother, I should. You think?"

"No, I think you'd better not." She pulled into the parking lot and up to the order board at Sonic. "What do you want?"

"Immy, I just want to date you. Nothing serious, just a date now and then."

"I mean for lunch!"

"Don't shout. Couple of hamburgers and fries, I guess. Iced tea."

She ordered hamburgers for both of them over the static-y speaker system and thought about the best way to get Ralph to spill. "Just a date now and then when I come in from the cold?"

"Don't matter if it's cold or not. But yeah, just a date."

"What was in Xenia's purse?"

"I don't think I'm supposed to say."

She laid her hand on his arm and leaned her face close to his. "Pretty please?" She tried to pucker her lips seductively. It must have worked because he closed his eyes and leaned toward her.

"Here's your order."

They both straightened while the server hooked the tray on the driver's side window. Immy let Ralph pay for the lunch, since she was running very low on cash. They ate in embarrassed silence for a few minutes, then both spoke at once.

"I didn't mean …"

"That wasn't …"

"You go," said Immy.

Ralph swallowed a fistful of fries and took a swig of tea. "I like you, Immy. I always have. I just want you to give me a chance." He looked at her. "And I think you should take those black things off your face."

Immy sighed. She might have to give up on the beauty marks. Maybe she could find a fat suit. "There are certain facts I need to know, Ralph. I need to clear my mother's name."

"The chief says you and her should pay for the fire damage to the girls' room."

"I can't do that. It probably costs a ton. Look, if you could help me pay for that, I could go out to dinner sometime, maybe next week." Maybe the heat would be off by then. "Do you think it's safe for us to return home now?"

"I don't know about that. We don't know who killed your uncle yet."

"I thought you thought Xenia did it."

"Because she has Hugh's driver's license and credit card doesn't mean she killed him, that's what Chief said."

Immy almost grinned. She had done it. She had sweated the details out of Ralph. He realized what he had said a few seconds later, though.

"Hey, I didn't tell you that, OK?"

Now Immy grinned, but just a little. "OK, but why don't you think she did it?"

"Why would she go back there to see him if she knew he was already dead? She told Frank she went to try and get her back pay, so it looks like she didn't know."

"But she told Frankie she talked to Hugh days after he was dead."

"How do you know that?"

Now Immy was confused. Hadn't Frankie said Xenia went to see Hugh right before her crash? No, he'd said he assumed she said that, but he didn't seem sure. Immy wasn't sure of anything either.

"I'd better be going, Ralph. I'll drop you back at the station."

On the return trip she promised Ralph to have dinner with him next Friday. That was a week away. Anything could happen in a week.

Twelve

Immy opened a can of chili and set it on the hotplate for their supper. She had tried to return Baxter's truck keys, but he didn't answer the door. She had left the keys on the left front tire. Everyone in Saltlick did that. Immy didn't know if people did it in other places.

It had felt good to get out of her undercover clothes and back to her real life.

Since her mother was on the other side of the bed, Immy sat on the side next to the hot plate so she could watch it.

Hortense simultaneously watched TV and read through the Wymee Falls newspaper Immy had bought on the way back to the Finest. Hortense had always loved to page through newspapers, even before she and Immy had made it to the local crime page.

Immy picked up a section her mother had discarded. It was the sports section and didn't interest her much. Then she reached for the front page Hortense had laid aside — and gasped.

"That's the car!" She pointed at the picture of an automobile on the front page. Above it the headline proclaimed BANK ROBBERS FOILED BY MYSTERY WOMAN.

Hortense rolled onto her side to look over Immy's shoulder. "What car?'

"That car was tailgating me yesterday."

The article told of a daring daylight bank robbery in Wymee Falls. The bank was held up by four youths who fled in a dark-colored SUV. They were apprehended at the edge of town with a flat tire, and all the stolen cash was recovered.

"She threw that thing at us out her window," one of the robbers was quoted as saying. The article went on to explain that a tire had been punctured with a letter opener, enabling the police to catch up to and arrest the accused felons. The license number of the older model van that disappeared from the scene had not been obtained by the police, who came onto the scene after the vehicle disappeared, they said. One witness said the van was red, another thought it was blue. Another was certain it was a pickup truck.

Hortense finished reading the article before Immy did and started talking while she tried to finish it.

"So you were tailgated by bank robbers? You're lucky they didn't shoot you. When someone tailgates you, let them overtake you. How many times have I told you that, Imogene?"

Immy gave up on reading the rest of the article. "That was my letter opener. Their tire was punctured by me."

Hortense gave that some thought. "You don't have a letter opener, dear. I believe the strain of a surreptitious life is affecting your mental acuity. Your synapses don't seem to be firing properly."

"My synapses are fine, Mother, better than ever. I was born for this life. I foiled a heist without even knowing it. Being on the lam suits me."

"Did you see the other article that … what's that smell?"

The answer to that became obvious as the sports section Immy had tossed too near the hot plate burst into flames with a soft whoosh.

Immy grabbed her phone from her purse and dialed 9-1-1.

"Nine one one. Please state your emergency," a cool female voice said.

"Fire!" screamed Immy. "Fire!"

"Can you tell me your location?"

The smell of burnt chili filled the room.

"A motel!" The name of the motel vanished from her frozen mind, then came back in a neon flash. "Cowlick's Finest. We're at Cowlick's Finest, and our room is on fire."

The first part of the reply was obscured by a beep. *Oh, great, my battery's dying.* "…immediately."

"What?" The crackling flames were spreading quickly. The wallpaper started to peel off in curls, and Immy choked on the smoke beginning to drop down from the ceiling.

"I said," the woman shouted, "if you're still in the room, you need to exit immediately. Did you hear me that time?"

The flimsy headboard, then the bedspread caught fire, and Immy jumped away. Hortense wasn't on the bed any longer. Where was she? The curtains started flaming. The fire's roar intensified.

"You don't need to yell." The phone beeped again. Immy couldn't see Hortense anywhere. The fire seemed to gain new life, and Immy realized Hortense had opened the door. The new air from outside fed the fire, and it renewed its assault even stronger than before.

The operator assured her that firefighters were on their way. She also suggested again, strongly, that they exit the building.

Immy didn't need any more urging. Hortense was already outside, gripping her purse. Immy grappled in the smoky darkness for their suitcases, grabbed them and lugged them out to join her mother.

"The chili," said Hortense, shaking her head. "The lovely chili." A tear coursed over the bump of her cheek, ran across her chins, and disappeared into her blouse. It left a track in the soot on her face. Immy looked down and saw that their clothes were covered with a fine layer of ash. Smoke billowed out the open door, and flames licked out after it. Even outside, the voracious fire was loud.

"But we're OK, Mother. Try to look on the bright side." *That's what Mother always says.*

The local fire engine careened around the corner, straight to their unit in the back of the motel. Sturdy, heavily clothed firefighters jumped down and ran through the door Immy had left standing wide open. The smoke spilling out into the sunshine carried the scents of burning wood, wallpaper and furniture with a hint of chili.

The two woman scurried to get well out of the way of the busy firemen.

A confusing, complicated orchestration took place, with a huge hose snaking into the room, and firefighters rushing in and out. More vehicles drove up, one of them the Fire Chief's car. Two of the men started knocking on the doors of other units and telling the occupants to vacate. In about half the units, dazed looking people stumbled out.

Immy's body started to tremble belatedly in the aftermath of the emergency. She noticed tremors beginning to come from her mother, too.

When one of the firefighters got to Baxter's door, there was no answer. His truck was gone. The fireman banged harder, shouting, "Fire! Fire!"

The manager had appeared, an older, infirm-looking man wearing a brown sweater laced with holes. The fireman at Baxter's door addressed him. "Is anyone in this unit?"

"I don't keep track of who's here, but I know one of their trucks is gone. The other one's right over there." He pointed to another truck beside the space where Baxter's had been.

From where Immy and Hortense stood, well away from the action, they could make out the manager and the firefighter talking to him, but the smoke smudged their view of the doors to the other units.

After some more vigorous pounding at Baxter's unit, the first one signaled for help from another firefighter. Together, they chopped a hole in the door with their axes and ran inside. Immy heard an outraged yell.

"What the fuck y'all think you're doing?

"Clearing the premises. Get out. There's a fire in the building."

One of the firemen exited, pulling a struggling man, string-bean thin, by his elbow.

"Let go of me you ..." the skinny man started coughing when he breathed the smoky air outside his unit.

The fireman remaining in the room stuck his head out and told his partner to call the police. "Looks like someone might be fixin' to make meth in here," he added.

"Let me go. I have rights. Y'all can't do this!" The guy squirmed and twisted, trying to get out of the fireman's strong grip.

"You're staying right here until the cops come," he said.

"Cops," Immy whispered to Hortense, urgency in her hiss. "We'll get hauled in if we stay here. I'm not sure Ralph could get us out of this. Or would."

"Imogene, do you really think we should persist in evading the authorities? I'm not certain that's judicious."

"Well, it sure isn't judicious to hang around here. Ralph told me that we're on the hook for damages at the police station from the fire I set there. I'll be in the papers as a serial arsonist. I'll bet the penalty for multiple fires includes time inside." She dragged the suitcases and tugged Hortense toward the salt cedar and scrub oak woods bordering the back parking lot on the edge of the cow pasture.

"Where are you going, Imogene?" Hortense questioned her daughter but followed meekly, her energy spent.

"I don't think we can take the van. We'll be seen by the authorities if we try a getaway in it. We'll have to leg it."

"I suppose you're right." Hortense cast a glance back at the van, then continued to trudge after Immy away from the commotion. "It seems we are effecting our getaway, as you call it, without detection."

When they reached the dense growth, Hortense slumped against a tree trunk that was thick enough to hide her, while Immy crouched behind a bush so she could observe the chaotic scene through its leaves. If her mother's knees felt as weak as hers, Immy knew why they were both sitting. She gulped the clean air. In spite of the stink that clung to their clothing, it was easier to breathe away from the smoke that continued to roll from their destroyed room.

The crew played a hose on the flame for a while longer and soon announced that the fire was under control.

"This unit has to be closed," one of the firefighters shouted to the manager, who seemed to be a little deaf. "You'll need to rip out the carpeting and change the furniture. Smoke damage. And if that dude was making meth in there, that's going to be whole other story."

"We wasn't makin' no meth," the skinny guy hollered, still being guarded by a firefighter.

The manager shrugged his thin shoulders and took a few steps toward his office.

"Making meth? In Baxter's unit?" said Immy. "You know, Baxter did have a sack full of that stuff you have to sign for."

Hortense gave Immy a knowing look. "That would be pseudoephedrine. It seems your friend was contemplating manufacturing methamphetamines."

Immy remembered an empty shed in Saltlick that used to smell bad occasionally, until it exploded one night. All four walls blew straight out. Talk was, that shed had been a meth lab. She didn't detect the odor here, but with the smoke, maybe she wouldn't be able to. Or maybe they weren't making it. She didn't want to believe Baxter was dealing.

Chief Emersen's shiny Saltlick cop car screeched around the corner, lights flashing and siren blaring. It braked two feet from the terrified firefighter who jumped back, still holding the still struggling, suspected meth maker and yanking him back with him.

"Meth lab," said the fireman, motioning the chief to look inside the thin man's room. Baxter's room.

The chief came out quickly and tacked yellow tape across the splintered door.

"We'll call Wymee Falls to come process the scene," the chief told the motel manager. "It'll be up to them whether they bring HazMat in or not. Until then, you're closed."

"But when will that be?" The old man sounded on the verge of tears.

"They'll be here in the morning when they can see what they're doing."

The manager shook his head and slunk away toward the office.

Chief Emersen made a phone call, then snapped a plastic band around the skinny man's wrists and shoved him to the cruiser. Cowtail didn't have a police department, but Saltlick extended coverage to them, so Immy knew he would go to her hometown jail.

It took another hour for the commotion to abate and the people and vehicles to clear away from the parking lot. The residents of the other units retrieved their belongings and departed. Immy and Hortense squatted on their suitcases in the woods and slapped mosquitoes, equilibrium slowly returning to both of them. Hortense's suitcase cracked when she sat on it but didn't disintegrate further. It seemed too early in the year for mosquitoes, to Immy, but there they were. Maybe they lived in the woods in the winter and early spring, she thought.

By the time the coast was clear, darkness had fallen. Incredibly, the van was still parked outside the ruined motel unit. The chief had to have seen it. Maybe he figured they left it there and hoofed it somewhere when they heard the sirens, which is what they'd done. They just hadn't hoofed it very far. The chief should have known Hortense wasn't that much of a hoofer.

"Where will we spend the night?" Hortense asked.

That was such a complete role switch, it left Immy reeling and speechless. Her mother was asking her what they were going to do? Her mother had always told her what they were doing, even when Immy didn't actually do it. Immy's mind whirled, feeling clouded, as full of smoke as the motel room.

"Well, we could …" Immy started, then stopped. What could they do? "Let's consider our options, Mother. Can you think of any?"

"Sleeping in these insect-ridden woods is not an option. I need walls and a roof."

"Right, walls and a roof."

Hortense waited, looking almost patient. Immy looked around wildly. She needed to think for both of them and wished she didn't have to. OK, the immediate options were the woods and the motel room. Those were both out, so they had no options. Then she thought of the van.

"Hey …"

"Hay is for horses, Imogene."

Immy smiled. Her mother was showing some of her old spirit. "The van has walls and a roof."

"That it does, dear." A faint smile played on Hortense's lips. "Let us relocate it, however, before we domicile therein."

Immy agreed it needed to be moved, but her mother could domicile all she wanted. Immy was going to sleep.

Thirteen

Immy drove deep into the countryside, down a dirt road between a couple of fenced cattle grazing pastures, not far from a place called Bryson's Corner. She pulled the van off the road, into the mesquite trees, until the hood bumped the barbed wire that kept the cattle in.

"Do you think you can sleep in here, Mother?" she asked, but before Immy even finished her question, Hortense had already reclined her seat and slunk down. In fact, she was beginning to snore. The night was warm, so Immy thought it would be all right to leave the engine off while they slept, not needing the heater.

It was dark and quiet. The mesquite barely rustled in the light breeze, and even the insects seemed distant, but Immy couldn't settle down. She needed to check on Drew before she could sleep. She shook her mother gently. "Do you have Clem's number?"

Hortense startled awake, reeled off the number, and plummeted into slumber again. Immy decided to get out of the van to make her call so she wouldn't disturb her mother any more than she already had. *Mother must be exhausted,* Immy thought. She herself felt like a zombie.

Being a desperado sounded much more romantic that it really was, she decided. They'd been on the run for, what, two days now? No, three. They'd spent two nights at Cowtail's Finest, and this would have been their third. How much longer could they do this? Not much longer, especially if they couldn't find a place to stay. No more nights in the van, Immy decided, even though they had technically only spent a few minutes of the night in it so far.

Immy sighed and closed her eyes, picturing her own bedroom, wishing she were home with her daughter and her mother. It was only a single-wide, but it was home.

Well, she would at least call Drew and make sure she was doing all right. That would give her some measure of peace of mind. She opened her phone, bracing for its light in the darkness.

Nothing.

She shook it, closed and opened it two more times. The battery was dead. She had the charger with her, thanks to her foray back to the house, but now she lacked an outlet to plug it into.

Hortense awoke when Immy clambered back into the driver's seat.

"Is all this commotion necessary?"

"It is necessary, Mother, to check on Drew. My phone is dead, so I'm driving to Clem's."

"Do you think that's wise?"

"I'm not wise, Mother. You know that. You've always said so."

"I have not, not in those words. You are sometimes injudicious, and not always efficacious, but I haven't actually stated that you are not wise."

Immy turned the key and slammed the gear into reverse. "You just did."

Her mother's wistful look took her off guard.

"What?" asked Immy, idling the van.

"You are, in fact, very much like your dead, sainted father, bless his soul."

Those words made Immy's heart swell with pride. Hortense could not have paid her a bigger compliment. A smile sketched itself on her face as she turned the van around and headed to Saltlick.

Warm light from the windows welcomed them as they approached Clem's little two-bedroom house. He lived on the opposite side of Saltlick from their trailer. Immy hadn't driven by their own place, feeling it would be too painful to see her home and not be able to go in. Besides, there was more risk of being seen and nabbed if they drove all over town.

"Should we ask Clem for some refreshments?" asked Hortense.

"We'd better not," said Immy. "You know how Clem hates cooking when he's not at work. I assume Drew is getting cereal and sandwiches. I think that's what he usually eats at home."

Immy stopped the engine and went around to the passenger side to help her mother climb down. The streets were empty tonight. That was a break, at least.

The drowsy chirp of crickets sang them to the door. Far in the distance, a pack of coyotes yipped. Immy looked up and saw a full moon, its pale radiance filtered through the branches of the huge live oak in Clem's front yard. As far as she knew, this house had been in Clem's family for generations. That tree might have been a sapling when the house was built. It was a nice, sturdy stone house, if a little on the small side. She and her family probably had more room in their trailer, but it was a good, safe place for Drew to stay for a while.

Clem answered her soft knock and let them in. He took a step back at the sight of Hortense, still dusted with soot. Immy was dirty, too, but Clem had eyes only for Hortense. He threw the door wide and ushered them in with an old-fashioned bow. He was amazingly flexible for having such a large roll of tummy fat.

"You've managed to get away from the law all this time, haven't you, Hortense?" he said, his eyes following her entrance and shining with admiration. "How in tarnation did you do that?"

"I sprang her, Clem," said Immy, wanting some credit for all her trouble. "I've kept her safe." Except for a little smoke damage.

"You're a dear daughter," he said, patting her on the head like a dog as she passed him, or maybe a very young child.

"We had a conflagration," Hortense told him.

"I started a fire in our motel room," added Immy, "and my cell phone is dead. I wanted to see Drew and tell her goodnight, if she's still up." Immy wasn't going to say anything about it being past Drew's normal bedtime. These were not normal times.

Clem waved Immy into the kitchen and joined Hortense where she had collapsed onto his nubby blue couch. The springs groaned from the combined burden of the two heavyweights.

"Hi, Sugar," said Immy, giving her daughter a kiss on the top of her dear head. Immy plugged her phone and her charger into the socket on the kitchen counter to at least give it a few minutes of juice.

Drew giggled. "Are you talking to me or to these?" She pointed to the fort she was constructing on the scarred, wooden kitchen table.

Immy sat beside her and chuckled at Drew's joke. The child was building a fort with sugar packets. They were hard to stack and kept sliding off each other, but Drew was persistent in sticking with it. "That's funny, Drew, a good joke. Hey, I've missed you." She kissed the top of Drew's head again and inhaled her clean, innocent scent. She couldn't get enough of it. "Geemaw and I have to, um, be away for a little longer. Can you stay with Uncle Clem for a while more?"

"He's pretty fun. He makes me special Drew pancakes with the letter D on 'em."

It was good he was fixing meals for Drew, she thought. The kiss Immy planted on her daughter's cheek left a black streak.

"You sure are kissing a lot today. You look funny, Mommy. You're all dirty. Did you play in the mud?"

She told Drew she's been in some smoke, then went to Clem's bathroom to wash her face and scrub her hands. She brushed what she could off her jeans and top, but they would probably have to be discarded. The soot was ground into the fibers, it seemed.

After Hortense washed up, they left. Clem stood at his front door, waving goodbye with tears in his hangdog eyes. Drew stood beside him, waving, too. As much as Clem adored Hortense, he hadn't offered them anything to eat. *Strange man*, thought Immy.

The road blurred in front of Immy from her own tears at leaving her daughter. How much longer would it be before they could live like a normal family again?

She drove back down the same dirt road to Bryson's Corner and parked, and this time they both slept until the sun assaulted their eyelids, flooding in through the windshield, only slightly filtered by the stunted mesquite trees.

Immy yawned and stretched, then found a spot of especially thick growth to hide behind while she relieved herself. Hortense followed suit with minimal groaning during her squat. They both retrieved clean clothing from their suitcases.

"Do you think these can be washed?" Immy held her smoky clothes at arm's length as they dressed behind the van. The clothing felt greasy. There were no socks in her suitcase, so once again, she pulled on the dirty ones. She had thought she found two pair of sneakers on the floor of her closet in the dark, but she had ended up with one old sneaker, one new one, and her restaurant shoes. Ugly, black things, but comfortable. That's what she wore. No sense in looking completely bonkers with mismatched shoes.

Hortense sighed, handed her doffed garment to Immy, and shook her head. "That was one of my favorite housedresses."

Immy stuffed the clothing under the thick layer of dank mesquite leaves on the ground, and they both climbed back into the van.

"Now what?" asked Hortense, buckling herself in.

After Immy started the engine and looked at the fuel gauge, she answered. "Now we get gas." *And, I hope, a place to put a little more charge on my phone.*

They pulled into a service station near Range City. After sticking the hose in the gas tank, Immy headed for the door labeled Ladie's to use it and its outlet. She knew her mother would want to move that apostrophe when she saw it misplaced like that.

However, her phone wasn't in her purse. She dug through it in the dim light of the tiny cubicle, refusing to dump it on the sticky floor, but there was no phone. And no charger.

Aha! She had left the cell and the charger at Clem's, charging away on his kitchen counter, and she couldn't get it. He'd be at the diner now. She would just have to wait until he came home. She didn't feel like doing any more B & Es for a while. Smelling as smoky as she did, she couldn't hope to avoid detection. At least her phone should be fully charged by the time she picked it up.

While Hortense used the restroom—after commenting, sure enough, that the sign was incorrect and should have the apostrophe at the end of the word—Immy wandered the two narrow aisles of the attached convenience store. She picked up a can of chips and some licorice, two of her mother's favorites. Come to think of it, almost all the items on the snack shelf were her mother's favorites. Without access to a hot plate, they'd have to eat snack food. She got some beef jerky for protein. Not that they would be having anything approaching a balanced diet for a while. When her life as a desperado was over, Immy would be very good about eating a healthy diet, she swore.

Hating to think of what would be in it, but wanting to be up to date, she grabbed a newspaper at the checkout counter. She kept it folded while she paid in case her picture was on the front page. The clerk wasn't paying much attention to her, but a matching photo in the newspaper might get his attention.

"Where to now, dear?" asked Hortense as Immy started the engine and pulled out of the station.

"I don't know, Mother. Any ideas?" She had no idea how to go about finding Huey's killer anymore. Nothing was working. Everything she did seemed to make matters worse. "Why don't you see what the paper is saying about us?"

Immy didn't even know which way to turn on the highway. Back toward Saltlick? Or keep hightailing it out of there?

Hortense rattled the paper as Immy decided to head back to the scene of the crime.

"We don't seem to be mentioned on page one," said Hortense.

"That's a relief."

"Oh, I'm mistaken. There we are."

Immy pulled onto the shoulder abruptly, setting off horns behind her. "Where?" She followed her mother's finger to the first story under the fold. "Hey, they're giving us credit for busting a dope ring!" Immy's face almost cracked with her huge grin, it had been so long since she had smiled that big. She held up her palm, and Hortense returned her high-five. "They don't name us, though. It says two occupants, who started a fire accidently, are credited with the capture. We're heroes!"

"Heroines, technically," said Hortense, "but yes, we do seem to be minor local celebrities."

"Maybe we can come in from the cold now." She peered over her mother's considerable shoulder and noticed the date at the top of the page. "Hey, it's Saturday today. I wonder what Clem's doing with Drew."

"What has he been doing with her the other days? Her pre-school doesn't occupy all the business hours of the restaurant."

"I don't know. I never asked. Maybe he takes her with him to the diner. He'd better not be leaving her alone in his house."

"Shall we ascertain that?"

Immy was all for it. It was a place to go and something to do, anyway.

Fourteen

"Exercise caution, dear," said Hortense. "You don't want to be incarcerated for breaking and entering."

"You're right, Mother, I don't." Breaking and entering? Not trespassing upon the premises or something like that? What was Mother coming to? She was turning into a hardened criminal, her own mother.

They'd driven around Clem's block three times, and the neighbors next door to Clem had waved to them every time.

"Do you think we look suspicious?" asked Immy.

"It's a possibility. We're still rather grimy. Maybe we should wait until it's dark."

"If Drew is in there alone, I'm not waiting for dark." Immy drove up to Clem's house and parked. "I'll go around back. A B and E is less obvious if done from the rear."

Immy couldn't read her mother's expression as she climbed down from the van and started around the cottage.

"Howdy!" The neighbors waved again. *That makes four times. Aren't they tired of that?*

Immy waved back.

"I don't think he's home," the woman called.

Immy ignored her and kept going.

The back door wasn't locked. *So I'm not breaking anyway, just entering.* The kitchen was dark. She tiptoed into the living room and surprised a tawny cat whose weight would rival Clem's if it were human. The cat streaked down the short hallway faster than Immy had imagined it could. She hadn't seen it on their last trip here and surmised it was afraid of strangers. A quick search of the two small bedrooms and one bath told her Drew wasn't there. She breathed her relief, standing in the room Drew was obviously using. Three Barbies were propped on the pillow. They were all new ones. Immy wiped a sudden tear at the thought of Clem's kindness and indulgence. He might make a good step-grandfather some day.

She reluctantly left the temporary room of her daughter.

On her way out through the kitchen she spied her cell phone, still on the charger and still plugged into the wall. She had almost forgotten about it, but she grabbed it before leaving.

The neighbor yoo-hooed and waved again as she returned to the van and backed out of the driveway.

"Are you all right, dear?" asked Hortense.

Immy realized she was still shedding tears. "I miss Drew so much, and I miss our house."

"Maybe the criminal justice system no longer regards us as felons. We are credited with apprehending the methamphetamine makers, and you said the only transgression on our record is the destruction of restroom property."

"I foiled the bank heist, too. Maybe we should show up at the station for our medals." Immy's mood brightened. She drove slowly in the direction of the police station.

Hortense gave her a doubtful look.

"I was kidding about the medals, Mother."

Hortense drummed her fingers on the armrest, her eyes narrowed in thought. "You might be partially correct, though. There may be some amount of appreciation shown us. An article I read before we fled the conflagration said I was merely being held for questioning in Hugh's death. It intimated that I had never been arrested."

"What are you saying? You didn't need to be sprung?"

"I guess I'm saying that the breakout may not have been necessary, and your actions may have been precipitous."

"I busted you out for nothing? We've been on the lam for nothing?" Immy twisted the steering wheel and aimed the van for Huey's Hash. She was going to see Drew. If they got picked up and arrested, well... They wouldn't do that, would they? The local heroes—correction, heroines? But if, just if, she wanted to see Drew again one last time. In case Chief Emmett had a BOLO out on them, or even an APB, she pulled behind the diner, and they entered through the back alley door.

"Mommy!" Drew ran to Immy, stepping on the picture she had been coloring on the kitchen floor. "Are we going home now?" Her little chin quivered, and Immy's heart felt tight in her chest.

"Maybe. Where's Uncle Clem?"

"He went upstairs." She raised her eyes to the ceiling where Immy could now hear Clem clumping around Huey's wood-floored office.

"I suppose with Hugh deceased, he needs to do the ordering of the produce now," said Hortense. She pulled out the stool Clem usually used and hoisted half her rear end onto it. The other half didn't fit.

"He'll at least need to order sugar," said Immy. "The most recent shipment was stolen when Uncle Huey was killed, Clem said. I wonder what in the world the perp wants with that stuff, although maybe Clem already got some more." She glanced at Drew's lopsided structure on the kitchen table. "Drew is finding plenty to play with."

The stairs rattled with Clem's descent. He paused when he saw the two women, then broke into smiles when he realized one of them was his beloved Hortense.

"How's Drew been?" Immy asked, getting right down to the reason they'd come. Drew wrapped her arms around Immy's blue-jeaned legs and held on. Immy stroked her daughter's shiny brown curls. Drew's hair smelled clean and was brushed.

"She's been an angel. Haven't you, sweetie?" Clem stood behind Hortense, who was still perched on the stool, massaging her shoulders with his ham fists.

Drew buried her head between Immy's legs.

"You miss me, Drew?"

"Mommy." The child started to sob, and Immy made up her mind.

"We're going home now, Drew." The tears dried in an instant, and the sun broke forth on Drew's little face. Immy's heart lifted, too. "We'll pick up her clothes at your house later, Clem, after you close up tonight."

"How's the business?" asked Hortense.

Clem cleared his throat and assumed a serious attitude. "Perversely, it's been great." Immy thought he tried to impress Hortense with his words sometimes. "I think morbid curiosity is making people come in and check the place out. That's all right with me, though. It's better for your family if business is good."

Immy supposed that was true. Her mother was probably the owner now. She would have to find out about that. Maybe there was a *Moron's Compleat Guidebook* for inheritance issues.

Back in the van, Immy announced, "I have one more stop to make before we go home." She turned two corners and slammed the van into a slot in front of the police station. "Let's see what the score is, shall we?"

Fifteen

Immy pushed open the front door of the police station and held it for Hortense and Drew. Behind the glass partition, Tabitha stood when she saw them, her eyes wide, her pale eyebrows hoisted.

"Well, well, if it isn't Saltlick's Most Wanted," she said.

Immy ignored her. "We need to speak to the chief."

"Well, la di da." Tabitha's fear dropped, and her usual sneer reappeared. "What if he ain't in? You think he waits around here all day for you criminals to show up?"

Hortense stepped toward the counter. "I'll have you know we are not criminals. We are heroines."

"I always thought heroines looked better than that." Her thickly outlined eyes raked both of them, and she had the audacity to shudder. Immy wondered why some of the caked mascara didn't shake off her lashes. "I'll get Ralph." Rather than lift her phone and ring him, which Immy was sure she could do and would be lots faster, Tabitha left her cubicle and sashayed down the hall.

"Do we look that bad?" Immy whispered to her mother. "We changed clothes."

"You smell funny," said Drew. "Your hair smells like a barbeque grill."

They hadn't showered. Immy shook her hair into her face. Yes, it did remind her of barbeque, burnt barbeque.

The door to the hallway swung open. Ralph filled it. "Hey, Immy." Ralph gave her a big grin.

"We've decided to face the music," Immy said, squaring her shoulders. She moved close to Ralph, stood on tiptoe, and whispered in his ear. "And you're going to help with the fine for the station damage, right?"

Ralph looked puzzled for a moment.

"Use your influence, Ralph. I know you have it. And dinner Friday?" Immy whispered.

"Right. Right. Sure. I don't know what I can really do, though."

"Can't you use your sway?"

His face cleared. "Chief said you were supposed to get a commendation for breaking up the meth ring. He's got one of the ringleaders in there now."

"I think I also foiled a bank robbery. The car with the punctured tire? That was my letter opener."

"Wow." Ralph's admiration shone in his eyes. "That was you? They might put you in the paper, *The Wymee Falls Press.*"

"We've already been in it a lot this week."

"Mommy and Geemaw's pitchers were in the paper," piped up Drew, "but you better let them wash their hair 'fore you take another pitcher."

Tabitha returned to her station behind the glass as the chief and Baxter, of all people, came through the door. Baxter? Was he one of the ringleaders? The small waiting area was getting crowded with the two large men, one large woman, plus Baxter and Immy and Drew.

The chief stepped toward them, but Baxter did a double-take at the sight of Immy and her family. "It's great to see you here," the chief said. "I have good news."

Baxter tapped the chief's shoulder. "Could I talk to you in the back for another minute?" he said softly.

Chief Emmett gave him a look of disbelief. "All you've wanted to do since we took you in is leave." He shook his head and shrugged. "But sure, if you want to talk some more. Are you going to say something this time?"

They went back through the door, leaving Immy and her entourage to cool their heels another several minutes. This time, when Baxter came through the room, he avoided Immy's eyes.

"Hey, hi, Baxter," said Immy. "What are you doing here anyway?"

He looked up but didn't answer. He gave Immy a slight frown and rushed out, his head down.

The chief walked straight to Immy's mother, his craggy face grim. "I'm very sorry to have to do this, but I'll need to ask you a few more questions, Hortense. I've just been made aware of a new situation."

His tone made Immy feel cold inside. It didn't look good for her mother. What had Baxter told him?

"Does she need to lawyer up?" asked Immy. "Are you going to read her her rights?"

Hortense turned her head away from Immy before she rolled her eyes, but Immy knew what she was doing.

"I need to ask your mother a few further questions in light of new information, Immy. You may wait here if you want, and I'll talk with you later."

He ushered Hortense into the hallway but left Immy with a stern parting shot, "Do not use the restroom while you're here, young lady."

Naturally, that made Drew think of using the restroom.

"I hafta go, Mommy." She squeezed her legs together and bounced.

"We need to go home now, Drew," said Immy, relieved to hear the words come out of her mouth.

Tears formed when she walked into the living room with its worn carpeting and tattered furniture. She sank onto the faded plaid couch as Drew ran to the bathroom.

She knew she should straighten up some of the mess she had left on her foray for clothing and her cell phone charger, but sitting on her own couch felt so good. She decided to leave the suitcases in the van in case they needed to go on the lam again. The chief had looked so serious just now.

The minutes ticked by. No call came from the police station. The elapsing time could not be a good sign.

What could Emmett possibly be talking about with her mother? What new information could he have? It must have come from Baxter. She would have to worm it out of him somehow. Baxter couldn't still be staying at Cowtail's Finest, since the room he'd been in was destroyed or at least smoke damaged beyond use for the foreseeable future. So where was he? Back in Saltlick, Immy assumed. She would be able to work Baxter better without Drew along, though. In case she had to use, well, feminine wiles. So, what to do with Drew?

Then Immy remembered her mother saying that Immy had been precipitous when she had busted her out of the interrogation room. Maybe she had better wait to see if Mother got released and sent home. Maybe it was nothing, merely some details to clear up. Maybe the chief had found out more about Mother being in the diner when she said she wasn't. Maybe someone had seen her inside the diner, like Clem. Immy refused to think Mother could have killed Uncle Huey. It would all work out OK.

When Mother came home, if Immy still needed to help clear her, Mother could watch Drew while Immy tried to charm Baxter into telling her what he knew, what he'd said to the chief that set him off.

THE PHONE WOKE IMMY. She snatched it and spoke with a thick, frog-like voice. "Hello?"

"This is Chief Emersen, Immy. You can come pick up your mother now."

Immy glanced at the clock on the television. It was nearly two. She had slept four hours. It wasn't nearly enough to catch up on her sleep, but it was a long time for Mother to be questioned again. She called out to Drew, who was playing in her bedroom, and they drove the van to the station.

"I'm glad you and Geemaw home, Mommy," said Drew, on the way back to the house.

"You liked staying with Uncle Clem, didn't you?" She hoped it hadn't been a hardship on Drew, except for missing her mother and grandmother.

"It was OK."

"Is there anything you didn't like about Uncle Clem's besides me and Geemaw not being there?" Surely Clem wasn't a molester or anything. Was he?

"Jus' no peanut butter."

"That's right, Clem doesn't do peanut butter." He was, in fact, allergic to it, and the restaurant used other types of oils for frying. Some of their customers remarked on the different taste of their fried food. Some liked it, some didn't. "Well, you can have plenty of peanut butter now," Immy said as she parked the van before the station.

Tabitha gave a shrug when she saw Immy and Drew, but she lifted her phone without delay to tell the chief they had arrived.

Ralph, the chief, and Hortense all entered the tiny lobby one after another, like a mini-parade. Hortense looked drained but peaceful. Evidently she wasn't under arrest this time, either. Immy hadn't known how tensely she had been holding her shoulders until she felt them drop and loosen.

Chief Emmett turned to Tabitha. "Do you have the paperwork ready yet?" he said, impatience in his voice.

That set Immy thinking. Maybe Tabitha was slow at her job. Maybe the chief wasn't happy with her as the desk person. Maybe she could be replaced by Immy herself, in case the PI job didn't work out. She made a mental note to look into that.

Tabitha pushed a few sheets of paper through the slot under her window to the chief.

"What's that?" asked Immy. She didn't want to stay for any paperwork. She wanted to get Mother home and comfortable and fed. She was probably starving after all these hours in the station. Lunch time was long over.

"Ralph, you may do the honors," said the chief. He was trying to look serious, but a smile broke out when he looked at Immy.

Ralph beamed and handed Immy and Hortense fancy certificates of thick paper with lacy bordering. His fingers left little damp circles on Immy's. He took a deep breath and recited, "Please accept these commendations for service to the citizens of Saltlick and Cowtail and for courage and bravery in showing extra … extraordinary initiative." Ralph looked to his chief, who solemnly nodded his approval. A big burst of pent-up breath came from Ralph, and his shoulders lowered just as Immy's had. She knew he'd been tense about his speech.

"How wonderful," said Hortense. Her chins creased with her huge smile. "It's so nice to be recognized for our meritorious service."

"That's for exposing the meth lab," said Ralph, "although they hadn't started making any yet." The chief gave Ralph a dark look. Immy figured he wasn't supposed to tell them that.

The chief held a few more papers, though. "Now the citation," he said.

Hortense perked up even more. "A citation, too? Is there remuneration for reward?"

"Not that kind of citation, I'm afraid," said the chief. "This is a citation for destruction of public property, and a fine."

Immy and Hortense both gave him blank looks.

"The fire," he said.

Hortense tried to make the most of her five feet, two inches. "We did not start the conflagration at the motel, which is not public property in any case." She tried to hand the paper back to Emmett.

Mother needs to stop lying to the police, although we didn't start the fire. I did.

At least the chief looked sorry to be doing this. He looked tired, too. Deep lines outlined his mouth.

"No, Hortense. This is for the restroom fire in the station the day you were being questioned. I did get the DA to reduce the fine to a symbolic amount. You'll notice it's only five hundred dollars."

Five hundred dollars was symbolic?

"Why couldn't you get him to reduce it to no dollars?" Hortense asked. "That would be a superior symbolic amount."

"Couldn't do it, the DA said. I did try. I really did. I tried to get the charges dropped completely. The grand jury happened to meet this week, though, and they sent it on."

The chief looked so sad, so apologetic. Immy had a sudden thought. Was the chief sweet on Hortense, too? She did have nice hair. And dimples.

Hortense turned her back on him and swept out the front door, dragging Drew with her by the hand.

"Thank you for trying to get this dropped," Immy said. She believed him when he said he had tried to. "I notice you didn't hold Baxter. Was he not getting ready to make meth in the motel?"

"No, Immy, we didn't. We don't have any evidence for holding him right now, but I can't say anything further about that."

"Bye, Immy," said Ralph as she left the lobby. He held the door to the hallway for his boss, but the chief waved Ralph on and let the door fall shut behind him while he remained in the lobby.

Immy started to go, too, but the chief stopped her. "Just a minute, Immy."

She turned and waited. The chief paused, regarding her but not with unkindness. "There's something you should know, or rather, something I should tell you." He paused again. "I don't think it's a good idea for you to be hanging out with Baxter Killroy. He's under investigation for a couple of things."

"He's not that bad, Chief. He's never done anything bad to me."

"Please think about it. Remember I told you, and be careful, OK?"

Now what was that all about?

Sixteen

Immy's mother and daughter were waiting in the van. They drove home in silence, even Drew.

Hortense was the first one out of the vehicle and up the steps. Immy got their suitcases and dragged them up the porch stairs, but her mother stood blocking the doorway, her arms outstretched to prevent Drew from entering.

"Call the police, Immy," she said, still holding her hands up. "Don't go in. The robbers might still be here. Drew, get back in the van."

"What is it, Mother?" said Immy, clutching the suitcases to keep them from tumbling down the steps of the tiny porch. "Can I just put these inside?"

"We've been burgled. Get your cell phone. Now, Immy. It's possible law enforcement will be able to catch the miscreant or miscreants."

Alarmed, Immy shoved the suitcases down the stairs and dug her cell phone out of her purse.

"Give me the chief," she said when Tabitha answered. "This is an emergency, and don't you dare put me on hold."

For once, Tabitha gave Immy some customer satisfaction.

"Robbery in progress," Immy yelled when the chief answered.

"Where are you, Imogene?"

"At our house. Mother says there's a robber inside."

"A burglar, Imogene," said Hortense. "It's technically a burglar when we're not home."

"Sorry," said Immy into the phone. "Mother says it's a burglar, not a robber. Anyway, I think you need lights and siren."

"We'll be right there." Was that a heavy sigh she heard as he broke the connection? Did the chief not appreciate the lingo either?

CHIEF EMERSEN POKED HIS HEAD out of the front door of the single-wide.

"All clear, you can enter now, but your place has been completely ransacked. You'll have to go through everything and see if anything has been taken."

"Oh," said Immy, looking down at her shoes. She had a bad feeling that she knew what she would find inside.

The house was exactly as she had left it after her clandestine trip, foraging for clothing and her phone charger. She really should have cleaned the place up when she was there earlier today.

IT WAS BEGINNING TO LOOK AS IF spring would arrive soon. Immy and Drew sat on a blanket at the Emersen Memorial Park. The park was named after Chief Emmett Emersen's great-grandfather and was situated at the edge of Saltlick, next to the cemetery. The town dump, which had been added years later, was on the other side of the burial grounds, but the wind was right today, and the gentle breeze smelled fresh and felt like a caress. It stirred Immy's hair, newly washed, and rustled the tiny, bright leaves of the mesquite scrub at the edge of the clearing. The sun gave off the right amount of warmth, not hot, like it would be in another month or so, but just right.

Immy and Drew were sitting on an old blanket, finishing up a picnic of Hortense's chicken strips and mustard potato salad, washed down with Hortense's sweet tea. After the Chief left, they had tidied up. Immy worked so hard that she wasn't in as much trouble with her mother as she had expected to be for making and leaving the mess. Then Hortense had taken a brief nap, sent Immy for groceries, and started cooking, whirling around the kitchen like a Texas twister.

"Why don't you girls go have a picnic? I feel like baking a cake, so I think I'll stay here." She scooped food into the margarine tubs she habitually cleaned and saved, and stuck the tubs and an old, thin blanket into a plastic WellMart bag.

"Oh goody!" Drew jumped up and down, shaking the floor, enthusiastic about the idea. "Swings!"

Immy laughed. It felt good to laugh. She didn't know how long it had been since something had truly amused her. "Sure, Drew. Swings."

They had strolled to the park, Drew swinging the plastic bag and Immy her purse and the bottle of sweet tea that clanked with ice cubes. They were waved and hollered at by Saltlickians sitting on folding chairs in front yards. Old Mr. Jergens, without his teeth, gave them a gummy grin. His visiting grandchildren chased each other around the yard. Immy assumed his wife and daughter were inside preparing supper. The Yarborough twins, spitting chew in the dirt, played checkers on a card table set up in the shade of the old live oak, the canopy of which shaded the entire yard.

Sometimes Immy longed to leave Saltlick, but not today. These were good people, friendly people. Sometimes she loved them.

In the park, their repast complete, as her mother would say, Drew ran to the swings as Immy packed the empty tubs into the bag to take home and reuse.

A mockingbird sang in the mesquite bush near the swings. Immy fell into the rhythm of pushing a giggling Drew. The child adored swings and thought three hours was a reasonable amount of time to be pushed continuously. Four hours would always be better, though.

Immy was going to start a job working for a real PI on Wednesday, four days away. It made her happy to think that the detective had actually called her, although it seemed that was in a different lifetime. She hadn't forgotten, though. She should be able to pay the fine soon. True, it was technically an interview, but she figured she would probably get the job. No one could be more eager for it than her, and if the PI job didn't work out, she might be able to take Tabitha's job away from her. That would be fun. That Tabitha was so snotty.

"Want some relief?"

Immy jumped and whirled to see Baxter Killroy standing three feet away.

"How did you get here?" she asked, taking a step back.

"Walked. Didn't you?"

"I mean, I didn't hear you."

"The grass may be still mostly dry, but it doesn't make much noise, Immy." It was true, it was greening up a little. "Do you want me to push Drew for a while?"

He gave it to her again, that slow, sexy smile. She twitched inside. The fleeting thought of the chief's warning made her hesitate all of three seconds. She stepped aside and let him take over.

"Hi, Unca Baxxer," said Drew, twisting her head around to see him.

"He's not Uncle Baxter, Drew," said Immy. "He's just Mr. Baxter."

"Mixxa Baxxer?"

"That's right Sit straight so you don't fall." Uncle Baxter! Would that ever give people the wrong idea.

"What was the problem at the police station? Why wouldn't you talk to me when you were leaving?" Immy asked Baxter.

"I'm sorry, babe. I just flat out don't like that place. Makes me nervous. I wanted to get the hell out of there. What were you doing there?"

"We got a piece of paper for busting the meth lab in Cowtail. Then we got a fine for the fire I set at the station when Mother was there and I sprang her."

"Immy, I think you read too many pulp novel mysteries. How much is the fine?"

"Five hundred dollars."

Baxter whistled. Immy watched his lips pucker. They looked warm and soft.

"Yeah, but I might be able to pay it. I got a job offer," she said.

"Hey, I can help you with it. I came into some cash."

"Down," yelled Drew.

"Really? Down now?" Immy was shocked. Drew had never voluntarily gotten off a swing.

"Wanna go over dere inna sand box. Wif Germy." She pointed to the sand pile enclosed by four eight-foot railroad ties, where a little boy pushed a huge yellow dump truck. His watchful mother, an employee at the library, sat on the bench of the nearest picnic table reading a magazine. The boy, whose name was actually Jeremy, was in Drew's preschool. Immy lifted Drew off the swing, and Drew ran to the little boy and began helping him load sand into the bed of his toy truck.

Immy returned to her blanket, and Baxter sat beside her. Awfully close beside her.

"You remember our deal, right?" he said, his voice soft.

What deal? Oh, yes.

"You don't mention I was at the motel in Cowtail, and I won't mention that you were there," he said.

"But everyone already knows we were there. We got a commendation for exposing the meth ring. Did you know they were doing that in your room?"

"No, I had no idea." Baxter shook his head. "It's sad, isn't it? But I could give you the money for your fine, and we could still have a deal. What do you say?"

This was a little confusing. There must be something unethical about this, but she couldn't see just what it might be. It seemed like a fair exchange. He didn't want to be mixed up in something that wasn't his fault, and he was perfectly willing to give her the money for the fine. She sure would like to keep her first paycheck. Drew would need new summer clothes soon, and she might want one of the new tube tops she had seen in the

Wymee Falls WellMart a couple of weeks ago. And she did want to get her own car someday.

"Let me think about it, Baxter."

"Don't think too long, babe." He leaned back on his elbows and crossed his boots at the ankle.

That was enough thinking. "Well, OK. I could use the money."

"That didn't take long." Baxter sat up, lifted a hip from the blanket, and pulled his wallet out of his back pocket. When he cracked it open, Immy was astounded at the number of bills. Maybe they were mostly ones.

"You said five hundred, right?" He started thumbing twenties. They weren't ones.

Would it be rude to ask him where he got all that cash? After all, he worked as a busboy at Huey's Hash, and Immy knew Huey didn't pay all that well. Maybe he had another job on the side.

"Here." He thrust a stack of twenty-dollar bills at her, and she tucked them away in her purse.

They sat in companionable silence for a few moments, watching the toddlers play in the sand, then Baxter got to his feet. "I gotta go, Immy."

Probably to his other job, she thought. "OK. See you around."

"Hey, what are you doing tonight?" He smiled down on her. Immy reached out her hand, and he pulled her up. His hand was warm and lingered in hers. "Hmm?"

"I, I'm not sure." Why did her brain stop working around this man? "I'll let you know."

"Call me," he said and walked away.

"YOU DID WHAT? YOU TOOK MONEY from Baxter Killroy?" Hortense's good mood evaporated as fast as Texas rain on a hot summer day. "Have you taken leave of your senses? Has your cerebellum ceased to function?" She banged the metal cake pan she had just washed and dried onto the counter. Immy jumped. "What does he want in return? Tell me that."

"Nothing. Well, nothing new."

Hortense narrowed her small eyes. "What does that mean, nothing new?"

"Well, I already said I wouldn't tell anybody he was staying at Cowtail's Finest when we were there. So he wants me to keep doing that or keep not doing that. Not telling."

"I know what you're saying." Hortense gave a mighty huff. The air in the kitchen moved. "But what you're doing is aiding and abetting, plus lying to the authorities."

"You've never done that?" Ah, Immy had her there.

"Please don't bring that up. I don't care to revisit that lapse in judgment on my part. I have bared my soul to the police now. They know my every movement."

"You came clean?"

"If you insist on phrasing it that way, yes. I told Emmett I was at the diner the afternoon you were terminated by your own uncle and that Hugh and I argued about his actions." Hortense slammed the cake pans into the cupboard, grabbed the dish cloth and started wiping down the counter.

"You came all the way clean?"

"What do you mean?" She scrubbed harder.

"Did you tell the chief I was there, too?"

Hortense stopped moving. She turned toward the counter, dropped the cloth, and hung her hands by her side. "No, I didn't mention that, Imogene. I couldn't bear it if you were … were found to be … if you …" Hortense wiped the corner of her eye with the dish towel, something she never permitted anyone else to do. "How deep are we?"

Seventeen

Drew raced into the kitchen, wailing, before Immy could come up with an answer for Hortense. Immy thought her mother's question may have been rhetorical, though. Drew ran to her grandmother and hugged her legs.

"Geemaw, look." Her little face puckered as she thrust a headless Barbie at Geemaw. "I need a new Barbie."

"Drew," Immy began. "You have enough ..."

"We'll buy you a new one," said Hortense. "I'll buy you a new one."

With my money, since that's all we have right now. The pension check for this month is long gone.

"Mother, she doesn't need another one."

"Don't argue with me, little missy. Drew and I haven't been shopping together, just the two of us, for too long. You have plenty of currency on you, as you have just informed me. We'll have a portion of it now, please."

Immy heard her mother's unspoken addendum. It might be a while before Drew got individual attention from her Geemaw if she and Immy were jailed anytime soon.

She reluctantly handed over a couple of Baxter's twenties and turned off the television after they left. The trailer was almost completely silent, an unusual occurrence for daytime. The only sounds were some creaks while the floor settled after Hortense's passage and the gurgle of the hot water heater. Drew's play often consisted of loud conversation between her Barbies. Also, Hortense liked to keep the television on so that if anything important happened in the world, she wouldn't miss it. She hadn't been watching the morning of September 11, 2001, and would never make that mistake again.

Wanting to be prepared for her new job on Wednesday, in case she weren't in the big house, Immy pulled out her two precious books. There wasn't an index entry in the *Compleat Moron's* book called Duties, so after a brief ponder she looked up the page for Investigative Techniques. She needed to know how a PI investigates, since she would practically be one soon. The section on entrapment might prove useful.

A pounding on the aluminum screen door soon startled her out of her concentration. Ralph stood on the wooden porch, taking up most of the space.

"Hi, Ralph," Immy said, cracking the door open.

"Immy, I need to talk to you." He pushed through the door and entered the living room.

"Friday, Ralph. Next Friday is our dinner date. This is only Saturday."

"Huh? Oh, I'm not here about that. I need to tell you something, to let you know … something." He turned his cop hat around and around in his hands.

"Well, do you want to sit down?"

"Huh? Oh, sure." He sat in the recliner, filling it nearly as much as Hortense did, and Immy took the edge of the couch. Ralph cleared his throat. Twice. "OK, then. I'm not supposed to be telling you any of this, but I think you should know. It's nothing definite, so Chief didn't want to tell you, but you might not be safe."

In the ensuing silence, Immy wondered if Ralph knew the chief had warned her about Baxter. It had been a strange warning, because the chief hadn't said anything negative about Baxter not being safe, just that she shouldn't hang out with him. But she had to stick to her deal with Baxter. She wasn't a rat. She wouldn't sing like a canary.

"How much do you know about the robbery, about the night your father got killed?"

Immy sat back against the back couch cushion. She hadn't expected that topic. "I know he was shot during a holdup at the diner. He was half-owner when he died, but he didn't work there anymore. Dad had started being a cop years before that. The night he died he was off duty, looking in on his brother, my Uncle Huey, after the restaurant was closed." She also knew her father's death had almost destroyed her mother. "They caught the perps, and I think they're still in the big house."

"Huh?"

"I'm going to be a PI starting in a few days, Ralph. I need to practice the lingo."

"I see." His face said he didn't. Mr. Mallett would, though, Immy was confident. He was a real PI, a professional. She couldn't wait to start working for him. He might even help her find Huey's killer. "Immy, not all the perps, as you call them, were caught. At least Chief has never thought so."

"But the two men they arrested had all the missing cash. They were convicted, weren't they?"

"Yes, they killed him, mostly likely, and they had the money, but the diner hadn't been broken into. Hugh used his key to get in, and Louie's was in his pocket. Chief has always thought there was an inside man."

Immy was impressed that Ralph knew some lingo, too. "An inside man? Someone who worked in the restaurant?"

"Yep." Ralph's slow nod seemed sad. "Nothing we could ever prove, though. His buddies haven't ever ratted on him."

More lingo. "So do you suspect someone in particular?"

Ralph's eyes grew hard. "We sure do. Always have. Baxter Killroy."

"He was working at the diner back then? I thought he started bussing for Uncle Huey recently."

"He worked at the diner for a few years before the robbery, then left the area. I don't know where he's been lately."

"But you don't know he had anything to do with it."

"No, we don't."

Immy's mind reeled. She tried to connect the dots between Baxter, the old robbery-murder, and Uncle Huey. The picture her mind made didn't connect any of the dots, though. It looked more like a jumbled abstract. She needed to know if Baxter had helped kill her father.

Maybe she could find out. Baxter had wanted to get together tonight. She would have to be careful, if he were a dangerous criminal. Could someone with those eyes and that smile be dangerous?

"Thanks so much for telling me, Ralph." Immy stood up, and Ralph had no choice but to stand up, too, and leave. "I appreciate it."

"See you Friday," he said as he ducked into his cop car. He slammed the door and drove off.

Immy spied Baxter's truck idling around the corner as Ralph drove out of sight. She stood on the porch and waited. Sure enough, a minute or so after the cruiser disappeared, Baxter circled the block and pulled his pickup onto the grass.

"Hey, Immy," Baxter said, climbing out and bounding up the wooden steps. "I saw your mother and daughter leave."

"And I assume you just saw Ralph leave. Why are you spying on me?"

"Not spying, babe. I wanted to see you alone, so I had to watch until everyone left. You promised to see me tonight, remember?"

"I did not promise to see you, Baxter. You said to call, but I didn't say I would do that either." What Ralph had told her was going through her head. She was torn between believing Ralph's opinion of Baxter and those sexy eyes.

"You know you want to, though, right?" Baxter paused to squint and check his reflection in the small glass window of the inner door, then strolled into the living room and tossed his cowboy hat onto the coffee table. "We have the place to ourselves, right? How long?"

"They're buying a new Barbie. Could take a while." Now why had she said that? She felt like clapping her hand over her big mouth. She probably should have said they'll be back any minute. She wasn't thinking straight again.

Before she could form another thought, Baxter had her in a clinch and had taken her breath away with his hard, hot kiss.

One thing led to another, and Immy got caught up in the moment. Between gasps, she resolved to start grilling Baxter. Not quite yet. In just another minute.

"Baxter," she panted, "I need to …" She tried to make her head stop whirling as Baxter used exactly the right touch in exactly the right places. Her clothing was coming off, one piece at a time, almost like magic.

"There's something we should …" Lordie, Baxter looked good without his shirt.

Immy heard the familiar sound of the Dodge's wheezy engine, as the van pulled up in front.

"Quick," she breathed. She snatched their clothes from the living room floor and pulled Baxter into the bathroom. He resisted for a moment, but Immy overpowered him, her adrenaline surging from panic. She got the bathroom door shut and locked as she heard the front door open and Drew burst in, announcing with a triumphant shout the purchase of three new Barbies. Immy groaned. Three!

"What the hell do I do now?" whispered Baxter.

"Sh. I'm thinking." Immy pulled her jeans on and slipped her tee shirt over her head. Her shoes could wait. It wouldn't look odd to be barefoot. "Get dressed," she urged him, when Baxter failed to follow her excellent lead and just stood there, practically naked. The window in the bathroom was small, but Baxter might be able to fit through it. It faced the back yard, too. So, with dusk approaching, that would probably be the best way for him to leave.

"Imogene." Mother's voice sounded right outside the bathroom door. She rattled the knob. "Unlock this door, Imogene. Why is Baxter Killroy's truck in our yard?"

Oops.

Eighteen

"And what is his hat doing on the coffee table?" Mother demanded.

Baxter moved fast when he got going. Immy snatched his boots from the floor and handed them to him as he reassembled himself. He was fully dressed in a flash. Must have had some practice at this, she thought.

Immy looked at the window again and figured he might not fit through it anyway. His shoulders were kind of broad. The bathroom was silent, except for the dripping faucet. Ah, that might work.

"Get down on your hands and knees," she whispered, her mouth on his ear so Mother wouldn't hear. Immy pulled open the door of the cabinet under the sink and pushed Baxter's head inside. Then she unlocked the door and whipped it open.

"Baxter was helping me look at that leak under the sink."

"You can't look at it yourself?" Mother had never appeared more skeptical.

"He thought maybe he could fix it. You know how it's been bothering you." She tapped the back of Baxter's head, and he pulled it out of the cabinet. "Guess not, huh?" Immy said to him.

"Nope, I don't think I have the right tools."

Whew. He caught on fast anyway. Baxter got to his feet.

"Well, bye, Baxter," said Immy. "It was nice of you to stop by."

She couldn't read his level, humorless look, which she hoped meant her mother couldn't either. The meaning probably wasn't all that good.

Her mother didn't question her after Baxter left, but she was decidedly cool to Immy the rest of the evening.

Immy pretended to read her PI books, but she couldn't get Baxter's boots out of her head. She had only gotten a glimpse as he pulled them on, but she thought the heel of the left one might have a squiggly chip off the edge. One that might match the picture she had seen on television and in the papers of the print in the sausage that had killed Hugh. She needed a better look at the bottom of Baxter's boots. She hoped maybe she could do it without his taking them off next time. She was beginning to think she had no skills in the *femme fatale* area. She hadn't wormed a single piece of dirt out of him.

"TIME FOR CHURCH, IMOGENE," called Hortense. "Get up, Drew, time for breakfast and church."

Drew bounced out of the toddler bed she slept in next to Immy's twin and started tugging on the hems of the dresses in her closet, not able to reach the hangers high above her head. Drew loved Sunday because she could wear her fanciest dresses without argument from anyone, along with her shiny, patent leather shoes. Immy opened one eye.

"This one, Mommy. No, this one. Wait, this one." Drew settled on a yellow extravaganza with a jingle bell sewn into one of the many crinolines under the lacy, beribboned skirt.

Immy opened her other eye. "OK. I'll get it down in just a minute."

"No, Mommy, now!"

"OK, OK." Immy sat up and rubbed sleep from her eyes. She had felt Baxter's warm, hard hands on her body all night, even in her dreams. She had had a moment of regretful letdown that she was in her own bed when Mother called her. That wouldn't do. Shaking thoughts of Baxter out of her head, she got Drew's dress from the hanger, slipped it over her daughter's tousled head, and fastened the buttons in the back.

"Go tell Geemaw I'm not going to church today. I have something to do. Tell her to brush your hair."

Two minutes later Mother was at the bedroom door. "What do you have to do today that is more important than your immortal soul, little missy?"

Immy paused, one leg into her jeans, and scrambled for a satisfactory response. She had an idea she should do something about Baxter's boot but hadn't decided precisely what it was. Her job would make a good excuse. "I have to study some more for my new job this week. I haven't had much time for it with all these interruptions." A plan was forming.

"Humph." Mother was the only person Immy knew who could actually say humph and convey an exact meaning with her utterance. She could also say pshaw. No doubt, Mother was a marvel. "Next time, Imogene, don't dress Drew for church until after she's had her cereal and juice, please. Drew, come pick another frock."

Until they left for church, a short walk of three blocks, Immy leafed through *Criminal Pursuits* and pretended to read random passages as she pondered what to do. She probably didn't fool Mother, but Mother couldn't argue with Immy needing to prepare for her job. Aside from the excellent information on disguises, however, Immy hadn't run across anything that looked useful. She wouldn't need a disguise for what she had planned this morning. The police must be told about Baxter's boot. Maybe it would match the footprint and maybe not, but they needed to find out what she knew. She didn't want to phone in another anonymous tip. She thought she had better give them this critical, sensitive information in person.

She walked to the station, glad her route didn't take her past the Holiness Baptist Church. She did pass within a block of it, though, and she knew the windows must be open because the strains of "Jesus Calls Us O'er the Tumult" floated to her on the gentle morning breeze.

She could hear Mother's strong soprano voice over all the others. Immy pictured her mother singing with an angel's expression on her face. Hortense could cuss up a storm and fiercely defy Christian ethics when it suited her, especially in defense of her family, but she was strict about attendance in church on Sundays. Maybe, Immy sometimes thought, it was a balance thing. Going to church made up for sinning during the week, and the louder you sang, the more you could cuss.

No one was at the front desk when Immy entered the station. She was glad she didn't have to have a stare-down with Tabitha today. Ralph's voice called from somewhere back in the building. "Be right out."

When he entered the lobby he told her to come back to his office. "I'm the only one here today."

"You have an office?" Ralph didn't seem important enough for his own office, but Immy guessed he had to do paperwork somewhere. *The Moron's Compleat PI Guidebook* said that police work consisted of as much paperwork as street work. That must be where Ralph did his.

He ushered her into a narrow room mostly filled with boxes. A small desk was pushed against one wall with a chair for Ralph behind it and one for Immy in front. The space didn't seem big enough to hold Ralph, let alone both of them.

"This is your office?" asked Immy.

Ralph looked a little sheepish. "It used to be a closet."

Immy eyed the stacks of cardboard boxes lining two of the walls. "Looks like it still is."

"What do you need, Immy?"

"I just want to see how the investigation is going. You know, Uncle Huey's murder."

"You came over on Sunday morning to see how the investigation is going?"

"Well, to see if you have any new suspects."

"We have some."

"You can't tell me who they are?" Immy batted her eyelashes a little.

"Are your eyes OK?"

Immy quit the batting. "Yes, my eyes are fine."

"I can't tell you who we suspect. Privileged information, you know."

"Yeah, I know. I was wondering about the footprint. That's not privileged. It was on TV. It must have gotten leaked to the press."

"Chief released that to the press to help find the killer."

Immy took a breath. She didn't want to outright accuse Baxter. "You remember the subject of yesterday?"

"Huh?"

"You know, when you came over."

"I came over to tell you not to hang around with Baxter Killroy."

"Yes, that subject."

"I'm right, you know. You shouldn't."

Ralph wasn't getting this. A buzz sounded, and Ralph said, "That's the front door. Be right back." He paused in the doorway. "Don't touch anything."

"Of course not." As soon as he was out of sight, she grabbed a pencil and notepad from his desk and penned a note: Check boots of Baxter Killroy. Compare to footprint. Hugh Duckworthy Case.

If she had thought this out more thoroughly, she would have cut the letters out of a magazine. Lacking that, she block printed them as anonymously as she could. She managed to make three of the letters with her left hand. Immy left the note on the seat of his chair and walked out of the closet. She had trouble thinking of it as an office.

Ralph was talking to one of the Yarborough twins about a neighbor's rooster keeping him up all night. She waved and left as Ralph's mouth dropped open. "But …"

The door closed on his sputtering, and she walked toward home. Before she reached the corner, though, Ralph came out of the station with the Yarborough twin, and they both got into the old cruiser.

"Shoot," said Immy to herself. "They must be going to see about the rooster." But when Ralph returned he would discover her note. He couldn't fail to understand the clue, could he? She could deny she left it if she needed to. She didn't want to have Baxter mad at her. Something told her that would not be a good thing.

IMMY WAS INNOCENTLY, SHE HOPED, watching television when Hortense and Drew returned from church.

"Are you through studying for your imminent employment, Imogene?" asked Hortense.

"All studied out, Mother." Immy gave a sigh to illustrate her state of weariness. She rubbed her eyes for good measure.

Hortense didn't look convinced.

"Play with me, Mommy?" asked Drew. So Immy sat on the floor for a rousing game of Old Maid. Unfortunately, one Plumber and one Pilot were missing, so they had to be matched to each other. Immy never remembered which ones were missing, but Drew always did, which meant Drew usually won.

Hortense changed channels idly, always restless on Sundays when there were no soap operas.

Immy startled when Mother banged down the footrest of the recliner.

"Look. It's Xenia." She pointed to the screen, and Immy threw down her cards so she could move to see the broadcast. "On the noon news."

"Mommy, we're not done."

"You won, Drew. Let's watch this show. C'mere." Immy sat on the couch and pulled Drew into her lap. Drew squirmed out of her embrace and ran to her room. "I get another game," she called back.

A picture of an unconscious Xenia filled the screen, then the camera cut to the announcer. "New information has come to light," the Wymee Falls news anchor said, "in the murder of Saltlick business owner, Hugh Duckworthy. Duckworthy's driver's license and a credit card, both assumed stolen, were recovered from the purse of Xenia Blossom, who remains in a coma in Wymee Falls General Hospital after an anonymous tip, given sometime yesterday, according to Saltlick Police Chief Emmett Emersen. In our exclusive interview with Chief Emersen, he declined to say if she would be arrested and said he had no further information at this time. More details as we get them. Stay tuned to this station for breaking news."

An old photo of the chief loomed behind the news anchor's head. It was exchanged for the fresh one of Xenia in the hospital halfway through the report. It looked like her driver's license picture.

That was the info Ralph had let slip to her, that Xenia had Hugh's stolen license and card. Maybe Xenia did kill Hugh and also made the print. Immy hoped so. That would mean Baxter didn't do it. But Xenia was in a coma. There was no way she could be questioned. Immy wondered if someone had planted the items in her purse. No one had been guarding her room when Immy was there. Anyone who claimed to be a relative could see her. Immy had claimed to be a relative, and so had Frankie. Maybe that's why Xenia hadn't been arrested.

Would it do any good to visit Xenia again? If only she could find out who else had visited her. Immy no longer had the wig, but she had hats and sunglasses. She could be another cousin this time, Maggie instead of Millie. That might work.

Nineteen

"I have to go out, Mother. Incognito," said Immy.

"Now? It's Sunday. Haven't you stirred up enough hornet's nests?" Hortense said, not removing her gaze from the rest of the news program. "You'd better see the rest of this. There might be more developments."

"There won't be until Xenia wakes up, if she ever does." Immy had an awful thought. What if Xenia died? No one would ever know the truth. At least no one would know whether Xenia killed Hugh or not. Everyone would remain under suspicion forever. "I'm going to suss out a suspect."

"What suspect?"

"I don't know yet. Whoever planted the goods on Xenia. I can't see her killing Hugh, much as that would be convenient. According to Frankie, she thought she would be seeing Hugh when she went to see Clem, or when she said she saw Clem. I don't think either of them knew Hugh was dead."

"Unless Francis prevaricated to you."

"Yes, unless that."

HOSPITALS WERE ALWAYS SO COLD. Immy wondered if germ growth was retarded by frigid temperatures. If she were a patient here at Wymee Falls General, she would be hollering for extra blankets for sure.

Xenia was covered by only a sheet and a thin white blanket. She looked even paler than the last time Immy had seen her. The tubes still snaked into her arm, and the screens still beeped and pulsed. The one with the spiky up and down things was probably the heart monitor, Immy figured. None of the lines ran flat, so she must not be brain dead.

Immy looked through the drawer in Xenia's bedside stand, but it held only her purse, mostly empty, a plastic thing to throw up in, some latex gloves, and some sort of tape, maybe for bandages. A *Bible* had been shoved to the back.

What else in the room could hold evidence? A narrow locker-type closet yielded a plastic bag that seemed to hold the clothes Xenia had probably been wearing when she came to the hospital.

Immy gave a sigh and plopped into the chair by Xenia's bed. Frankie must have visited recently, because the chair was smack against the rail. Immy would bet he'd been holding her hand. She felt sorry for him. It must be hard to watch the one you love suffer and be tortured like this. Except Xenia looked peaceful, not tortured.

As that thought crossed Immy's mind, Xenia's face contorted. The heart monitor scrawled some extra jagged lines across the screen, and Xenia's eyes fluttered, then opened.

"Omigod!" they cried in unison.

"You," said Xenia. "What the hell are you doing here, Immy?" She raised her head and looked around the room. "Where did Frankie go?"

"I'm your Cousin Maggie. I didn't see him. Did you see him today?"

"Yeah, he was here when I woke up. I didn't know where the hell I was, and I don't have any cousins named Maggie."

"Do you remember your wreck?" asked Immy. "You rear-ended a combine on the way out of Saltlick."

"I remember a little bit. I know I was spittin' mad at Clem. He wouldn't give me my last paycheck. Hugh had told me to come back in a couple days, so I did."

Xenia's frown brought a smidge of color to her face. "Clem wouldn't tell me where Hugh was or nothin'. He made me so mad."

"So that's why you got in the wreck?"

One of the monitors fussed when Xenia shrugged and tried to shift in her bed. "I wasn't paying enough attention, I guess. I was powerful mad. That combine must have been going about five. I was so mad."

Immy gathered she had been mad.

"That Clem, he was acting all mysterious. He's as creepy as that turd Hugh if you ask me. I'm glad I don't work there no more. One of them has to pay me, though."

"So what exactly did Clem say to you?" said Immy.

"That he couldn't pay me. Something about assets probably being frozen."

Clem had told Immy he hadn't spoken to Xenia before her wreck. One of them was lying.

"What did he mean about assets being frozen?" asked Immy.

"I don't know what the hell he was talking about."

Immy wondered if Xenia could make up stuff about assets being frozen. Maybe not. Immy herself wasn't sure what it meant.

"What do you know about Frankie's family buying Uncle Huey's restaurant?" said Immy. "He told me his family wanted to buy it but Hugh wouldn't sell."

"Yeah, Frankie told me about that."

"How badly did they want the restaurant? Badly enough to kill?"

"What do you mean? I think they still want it. Hugh would never budge, though. He wanted way too much money."

"Frankie thought you had talked to Hugh. At least that's what he told me."

Xenia struggled to sit up. "Don't you believe anything that rattlesnake says! You know what he said to the cops? Do you?"

The heart monitor beeped frantically.

"Should I get a nurse?" asked Immy.

"That damn Frankie. We're through. T-H-R-U, through. He told the cops I might have killed Hugh. He said that for all he knew, I did it. Hell, I didn't even know the old bastard was dead until Frankie told me today. Wouldn't I know he was dead if I killed him?"

A nurse rushed into the room. "Are we awake again?" Her voice was hearty.

"I'm not friggin' deaf," said Xenia with a scowl.

"I'll bet we're hungry." The nurse seemed to have such a naturally loud voice that she couldn't possibly contain it or her cheerfulness either. Over the top, in Immy's opinion.

"Don't know about you, but I'm starving," said Xenia.

"I ordered you some lunch. You get Jell-O. Isn't that nice?"

Xenia made a horrible face.

The nurse bustled about, checking machines and tubes. "We've notified the Saltlick police. They'll want to talk to you after you've eaten something."

"I think I'll take off now. See you later, Xenia." Immy got up and scooted out of the room. She didn't want to be found at Xenia's bedside when the police arrived, although Immy would love to hear what happened. She looked up and down the hallway, trying to figure out a way to hang around and spy.

She didn't need a disguise for normal travel anymore, since she had come in out of the cold, but she would need one in order to spy some more at the hospital. As she passed the large trash barrel she had overturned when Frank and his Uncle Guido were in the parking garage, she whipped off the hat that had made her into Cousin Maggie and tossed it in.

She had to admit, the glasses and hats weren't working. She needed another wig or maybe a fat suit.

Twenty

Immy was in luck. The costume shop was open on Sunday, and it marketed a huge array of fat devices. She pawed through packages that promised to turn her into an obese cheerleader, opera singer, or member of a harem. Too bad there were no nurses or doctors. Any of those others would be too obvious and far too expensive for her purposes.

She kept looking. On a lower shelf she found a section of cheaper packages that concentrated on separate body parts. She settled right away on the Big Boobs N Belly package, liking the cheerful illustration of the chubby person on the label, then debated between Fun Buns and Buns of Foam. The Buns of Foam were a dollar cheaper, so she chose them. They didn't seem to come in sizes, saying "one size fits most." Wouldn't they make fat accessories to fit only skinny people? Why would people who were already fat need them? She hoped one size fit her.

"These foam buns are extremely popular right now," the sales clerk said between smacking her gum and bobbing her head so her large hoop earrings swung against her ample neck. Immy didn't think the poor girl would ever need any amplified body parts.

"Do you have a changing room?" asked Immy.

"You want to wear these right now? You're going to need bigger clothes."

Good point, a detail Detective Duckworthy had overlooked. Drat. "Well, do you have large clothing?"

"Are you kidding?" The clerk pointed Immy toward a long rack crowded with outsized clothing. Immy chose a pair of tan gaucho pants and a Hawaiian shirt in shades of blue, pink, and orange.

In the small, curtained space that passed for a dressing room, she strapped the Boobs N Belly contraption onto her torso, glad the weather hadn't turned steamy hot yet. This thing could probably get warm. The buns strapped on, too, and the clothes seemed to fit just right over everything. It was like they were made for each other. In Immy's experience, "one size fits most" didn't always work out, but she was glad it did now.

Before she left the shop, she thought to pick up another wig, this one of curly red plastic locks. She waddled awkwardly when she walked. If this was what being fat felt like, she pitied her poor mother.

It wasn't easy to fit behind her steering wheel, but she found that if she tipped the steering wheel up, she could do it. Now she had to hope she wasn't too late getting back.

Immy scored a parking space on the first floor of the hospital parking garage. *My luck must be changing,* she thought. *This is going to work out great.*

She breezed past the guardian at the reception desk, posing as Auntie Raylene this time. The woman did comment that Ms. Blossom had a large family but only gave her a glance. Sure enough, when Immy got to Xenia's room, her luck still held. Maybe she would pick up a Lotto ticket later.

The bed was empty, but she could hear Xenia talking to someone in the bathroom. Immy assumed the nurse was helping her to the toilet. Xenia was not having a good time, though, judging from her whiny tone.

Immy opened the locker, kicked the plastic bag to the back, and squeezed in just as the bathroom door was opening.

"There," shouted the nurse. "Don't we feel all better now?"

Xenia's grumble was too quiet to hear. Immy had a moment of worry. Maybe she wouldn't be able to eavesdrop on the conversation between the police and Xenia. Maybe she would run out of oxygen in this tiny closet. Maybe she would die here. Then she noticed the slits and decided oxygen wasn't going to be a problem. She could also turn her head so her ear was against the slits and hear Xenia just fine.

"I don't like vanilla shakes. I need chocolate. And give me some more friggin' blankets. This place is like a walk-in fridge."

The room no sooner grew quiet, presumably with the exit of the noisy nurse, than Immy heard Chief Emersen's voice.

"Oh, Christ," said Xenia. "What the hell do you want?"

"Good afternoon to you, too, Ms. Blossom. I assume you know my assistant, Ralph Sandoval."

"He's picked on me for speeding when I was hardly even over the limit," Xenia whined. She may have added the word jerk, but Immy couldn't quite tell.

"I'm going to ask you about the last time you saw Hugh Duckworthy and then a few more questions about the events leading up to your accident. Do you feel able to answer?"

"My mouth works fine." Immy nodded, silently agreeing with that.

Chief asked Xenia if he could record the conversation, and she ungraciously consented.

Immy could hear fine, but she didn't learn anything new. Xenia said she last saw Hugh when she quit, and he said he would pay her in a few days. She related the same story she had told Immy about Clem giving her the runaround and making her so mad she stormed off and hit the combine.

"You can't believe that lyin' asshole, Frank Laramie. Did he tell you I killed Hugh?" Xenia said when it seemed the interview was winding down. "I think he thinks I did, although why he'd think that, I'm sure I don't know. Maybe he's trying to mislead y'all. So did he tell you that?"

"I'm not at liberty to answer that," said Chief. "Do you have any reason at all to believe Laramie might have killed Duckworthy?"

A moment of silence. "I never thought of that," said Xenia.

Immy hadn't thought of it either.

After repeating all the same questions over again and thoroughly aggravating Xenia, the police left. Then Immy wondered how she was going to make a graceful exit. She hadn't thought ahead to that point. Everything had been going so smoothly.

Minutes ticked past. The closet got more and more uncomfortable. Immy didn't have room to shift her weight, and it started getting warmer and warmer. More minutes. Hotter still. She tried not to pant, so Xenia wouldn't hear her, but sweat was dripping onto the plastic bag at her feet, making tiny plinking sounds. She moved her foot and the plastic bag crinkled.

"What the hell is that?" called Xenia. "Is there somebody in there? This place have rats?"

Xenia must have rung for the nurse because one yanked the metal door open a few minutes later.

It was the loud, cheerful nurse, but now she was loud and puzzled. "Well, what do we have here? What on earth …?"

Immy tried to get out of the closet but found she couldn't. Her fat suit parts were wedged in so tightly she couldn't budge. The Buns of Foam were squishable, but the Big Boobs N Belly was one piece of hard plastic, and there was not an inch of give to it.

"Get out of there," the nurse commanded, still loud but no longer cheerful.

"I can't," said Immy, on the verge of tears. "I'm stuck." She struggled, pushing against the sides of the locker, knocking her wig askew.

"Give me your hand."

The nurse tugged on her until Immy thought her wrist would snap. "Ow!" Immy yelled. "That's not going to work."

"How did you get in there?" asked the nurse.

"And when?" said Xenia.

"While you were in the bathroom, I squeezed in here. But see? There's this metal lip thingy I can't get past. It's gouging my Big Boobs N Belly."

"Your what?" said the nurse.

"That's the brand name. I'm wearing fat suit stuff. My buns squish, they're Buns of Foam, but the front piece doesn't."

The nurse rapped her knuckles on Immy's fake belly. "Yes, I can see that."

A howling arose from Xenia's bed. "It's Immy, isn't it? You look so ..." She couldn't finish. She was laughing too hard to speak.

Immy started to panic. Her heart thumped, and she couldn't get enough air, even with the locker door open.

"Get the Jaws of Life!" yelled Immy. "Cut me out of here! I can't breathe!"

Now the nurse started giggling, a high annoying gurgle. "You can't use Jaws of Life for this." She gurgled some more. Immy didn't think it was very professional of her. "Scissors won't cut that plastic, pretty sure. I'll see if I can get an on-call surgeon from ER. He'll be able to get through this thing." She gave Immy's belly another whack with her knuckle and whisked out of the room.

Twenty-One

What hurt the most was the way Mother laughed when Immy got home and related the events of her day. She sounded just like Xenia and the nurse. And the ER doctor.

"It wasn't all that funny," Immy said.

Hortense wiped tears off her dimpling cheeks. "I'm just sorry you didn't bring them home. I would like to have seen the costume in its entirety."

"You couldn't see it anyway. It's in pieces. That young surgeon had to saw the plastic into three pieces to get me out. He laughed so hard I thought he was going to saw me in half. I was exposed right there in front of him, and he was young—and cute, too."

Hortense had quit hooting, but she still shook, not unlike a bowlful of jalapeño jelly, in Immy's opinion. "I'm sure he sees female bodies a lot in his line of work. You could have brought home the Buns of Foam, couldn't you?"

"I could have been seriously injured."

"Imogene, you look so much like Drew when you pout." Immy's mother gave a final snort and returned her attention to the television.

"Are they arresting Frank again?" Immy asked when she saw him being led into the police station in handcuffs.

"No, I think they're saying something else happened. This picture is old footage from his last time. Be quiet and listen."

They seemed to be showing the only pictures of Frankie they had. He was being sought by police for questioning after having fled the area.

"My gosh," said Immy. "Frankie's on the lam."

"He has eluded the authorities, yes," said Hortense.

The announcer droned on. "Laramie is regarded as a person of interest in the bizarre murder of Hugh Duckworthy, proprietor of the Saltlick eating establishment, Huey's Hash. Laramie is said to have underworld connections and is considered dangerous. If sighted, please do not approach, but notify the police in Saltlick." He gave the phone number.

"Uncle Guido," murmured Immy.

"Uncle Huey, not Guido," said Hortense.

"No, Guido is Frankie's underworld connection. I heard them talking at the hospital last time I was there. So, with his running away, and the cigarette butt …"

"What cigarette butt?"

"I found his cigarette butt at the diner and grassed."

"You what?"

"I tipped the cops. That's why they hauled him in the first time, but they couldn't break him. Then he fingered Xenia, which is stupid. She didn't even know Huey was dead. Like she said to me, if she killed him, she would know he was dead, right? I need my list. Where did it go?"

Immy had left it in the living room, she was certain, but after much searching, she found her list in her top dresser drawer, no doubt moved there when Mother "straightened up." She added a check mark after FRANK LARAMIE under the heading, SUSPECTS, to indicate he had two strikes against him. The other names listed so far were XENIA BLOSSOM and BAXTER KILLROY, but she didn't really suspect either of them. She would have liked to add HORTENSE DUCKWORTHY, so her list would include everyone the police suspected, but it wouldn't do to have Mother find her name there. Obviously, Mother was the person who had put the notebook in Immy's top dresser drawer. She would have to think of a code name for Mother. She needed a book on codes.

Should she list Uncle Guido, GUIDO GIOVANNI? That would be Frankie's mother's brother of the El Paso Giovannis. No, he seemed to enter the picture after Huey's murder. If someone else got bumped off, though, he'd go to the top of her list. Frankie had said he wanted him to do just one more job. Did that mean he'd done one recently, or were they talking about jobs he did back in Sicily?

Immy realized that she hadn't heard anything at all about Baxter being questioned. She had left the note for Ralph about his boot and everything. Why hadn't he been grilled?

She looked up the non-emergency number for the Saltlick police station, recognizing it as the same one just given on TV for tips. Tabitha put Immy on hold for ten minutes. She probably didn't even tell Ralph there was a call for him for nine minutes.

"Hey, Immy," he said. He sounded so happy to be talking to her. "How's it going?"

"I was wondering …"

"I've got a great place picked out. It's new. My cousin went there over the weekend, Saturday night he went, and he said the servings are humungous."

"Sounds nice, Ralph, but I was wondering …"

"It's not fancy or anything. Jeans are fine. I guess you could dress up if you want to, but you don't …"

"Ralph! Did you see that note I left … uh, someone left in your chair? I saw it when I was there."

"What kind of note? In my chair? Let me look."

Immy heard his chair squeak.

"Well, I'll be. There's a note here. I've been sitting on it."

Immy clenched her eyelids tight. It seemed to help keep her mouth shut.

"Huh?" said Ralph.

A small growl of frustration must have escaped from her throat. "What does the note say? I didn't read it."

"I thought you said you left it."

"No, no, I just saw it there. Well, I'll talk to you later, Ralph. Looking forward to Friday night."

Maybe now someone would find out if Baxter's boot had made the footprint.

IMMY WANTED TO TRY AN ANONYMOUS note one more time. Surely it would work this time. She had tried to warn Clem in conversation that Frankie's Uncle Guido might be gunning for him, but that hadn't had any effect. The more she thought about it, the more she thought Clem must be on Guido's hit list. Frankie had been asking for him to whack someone when she overheard them, and if Frankie had fled town, there was a good possibility he was the murderer of Hugh. He might have known all along that Xenia talked to Clem, not Hugh, right before her accident. Had he been trying to mislead Immy by pretending he thought Xenia talked to Hugh? Had he been thinking of fingering his moll for the crime all along? What a dirty, rotten rat.

So, if Guido was set to "do" Clem, Immy needed to make sure Clem knew about that. Maybe he could get police protection or hire a body guard.

It was Monday morning. Hortense had left to take a tearful Drew to preschool. Drew had realized, while gathering her things for school this morning, that she had left one of her new Barbies at Clem's. How she could keep track of all of them, or even tell them apart, was beyond Immy. But Immy thought she would go to Clem's, sneak in, get Drew's Barbie, and leave a note warning Clem that his life was in danger. That was a whole mission.

Hortense had said she was going to drive into Wymee Falls to grocery shop after she dropped Drew, so Immy would probably have enough time, but none to waste.

Immy shuffled through the magazines on the coffee table: *House Beautiful, Southern Living, TV Digest* ... ah, here's what she needed, *Reader's Digest*. Hortense never picked that one up again after she read the jokes, but she leafed through the others until the pages curled. Immy put on a pair of rubber dishwashing gloves and set to work with scissors and Drew's school paste, putting together her message. She had learned her lesson on the note for Ralph, and she would be better prepared this time.

The note should be dire, ominous, and maybe a little illiterate so the author couldn't be guessed. Immy decided on her wording:

WARNNING

A HIT MAN HAS A CONTRACT OUT ON YOU

BEWEAR FOR YOUR LIFE

SEEK PROTECTIoN FoR YoURSELF

She found most of the letters she needed in large titles for articles. The only letters she ran short of were capital O's. That was good. She tacked them onto a piece of plain white paper, which she hoped would be untraceable, and made the letters a little crooked on purpose. The anonymous notes she had seen on TV were always a little crooked. She admired her finished note for a moment and got her shoes on while the paste dried.

Time for another B and E. If the PI thing didn't work out, maybe she would make a good criminal.

It might be easier to break into people's houses at night, Immy thought. She had had such good luck at her after-dark B & Es. During the day like this, she would have to be extra careful she didn't get caught. This was the time of day when Clem was at the diner, though, so this was when she would have to do her deeds. She couldn't very well break in while he was at home. Also, Hortense was occupied for a while, and she didn't leave home all that often.

She remembered Clem's back door had been unlocked last time she broke in. It should still be unlocked today. People either always or never lock doors, she figured. She thought she should dress as if she were going out for a stroll. She rarely strolled, but some people did. Immy pondered her closet for a few minutes. A jogging suit would be perfect. However, lacking a jogging suit, she wore jeans, tee shirt, and sneakers, which was no different than her usual daily dress. Anyway, she wasn't going to jog, she was just going to be strolling.

She strolled around Clem's block three times before the coast was clear. The other times, the neighbors were out planting flowers in the front. They waved as she passed. The third time, no one was in sight. She dashed around to the back. To her relief, she found that the door was again unlocked.

He really ought to lock it. No telling who might get in.

Immy looked for the huge cat she had seen last time she was there, but it must have been hiding. The first thing she did was prop her anonymous note next to his coffee maker on the kitchen counter. Then she started looking for the Barbie. Drew had said this one was Superstar Barbie and she was attired in a floor-length fuchsia frock. That shouldn't be too hard to spot. Drew didn't know the word fuchsia, but there was a TV ad that played frequently for Superstar Barbie, one of the newest models.

Fifteen minutes later, Immy changed her mind. There was no way she was going to find Superstar Barbie. Clem's little stone house was tidy and clean, and there weren't many places a doll like that could hide. She had found the cat under Clem's bed, but no Barbie. She was surprised to see a sugar packet fort standing on his kitchen table. He must have been reluctant to take Drew's handiwork apart. Maybe he thought she would be back soon, and Hortense would come with her. Maybe Drew had even made him promise to leave it. That was something Drew would do.

When Immy returned home, Hortense wasn't there yet, but the chief was. His shiny cruiser idled in the front yard, and Emmett sat behind the wheel, drumming his fingers on his steering wheel.

"How soon will your mother be back?" he said, getting out of the car.

"What now?" Immy stopped beside him, trying to assess his mood. "Did you find the killer? Is it Baxter?"

Emmett narrowed his eyes. "Why do you ask that?"

"Well, you yourself warned me about him. I just thought maybe …"

"We matched Baxter's boot heel to the print left in the sausage, but there's no evidence he killed Hugh. Baxter repeated an accusation, though, that I have to check out."

An accusation to check out with Mother? An accusation *of* Mother?

With atrocious timing, the green van swung around the corner and pulled up beside Emmett's cruiser. Why couldn't she stay away until Chief left so Immy could hide her?

"Hi, there, Emmett." Hortense smiled at him as she climbed out and went to the rear of her vehicle to fetch the groceries. "You're just in time to help."

She certainly seemed chipper, Immy thought. Of course, having a house full of new groceries always cheered her up.

"Come over here and help carry," Hortense ordered the police chief. He walked around to the back of the van, and she thrust two grocery sacks at him.

He gave her a chance to put away most of the foodstuffs, then drove away with Hortense in the back seat. Again.

This stuff is getting old. I need to do something.

Immy decided Mother needed to lawyer up. She called the attorney Hugh had used for the restaurant, a corporate attorney in Wymee Falls by the name of Stinton Ogilvie Braden. It only took a few minutes to get through to him, and he agreed to meet Immy at the Saltlick station. Immy drove the van there, although she knew she would beat him by at least twenty minutes.

While Immy cooled her heels in the lobby, Tabitha shot suspicious looks her way. It was no wonder, Immy thought. If she herself saw someone get dragged to the station and questioned as much as Hortense, she might start to consider the family had some bad blood in it. But this was her family, the Duckworthys. There was no bad blood, dammit. There couldn't be. That might mean Drew would have gotten some, and Immy knew Drew didn't have bad blood. Drew had stubbornness and precocity and her own ideas that sometimes didn't make much sense, but her sweet daughter had no bad blood.

Hortense kept a picture of herself and Louis, her late husband, on her dresser. It was Immy's favorite, and she looked at it often. It was a shot of them hiking Palo Duro Canyon in Hortense's younger, slimmer days. The wind caught her hair just as the camera snapped. Her face was turned slightly toward Louis, and his was tilted down toward her. Such a handsome couple, and they looked so happy.

For the most part, they were happy together, as Immy remembered. The only big dissention she recalled was that Hortense hadn't wanted him to go into law enforcement. She had relented, though, as his career progressed and even bragged to people about him being a policeman and, eventually, a detective.

Her life was shattered when he was killed. Immy would always remember the way Hugh had had to pry her fingers off the railing of the hospital bed to get her out of the room so his body could be removed. It was after that Hortense started eating. No one in the family tried to stop her. She refused to talk about her husband for several years. Immy hadn't said the word Daddy in front of her for three years.

Then, two years ago, Hortense decided to celebrate his birthday. She baked his favorite cake, chocolate yellow marble, and slathered thick chocolate frosting over it. She lit candles and made Immy join her in singing "Happy Birthday to Daddy." Immy managed a few bites of cake, and Hortense ate the rest, or maybe she threw it out. At least it was gone the next morning.

Immy had shut herself in her room after the weird, uncomfortable non-celebration and cried herself to sleep, sure that her mother had finally lost her mind.

But after that occasion, the subject of her father, Hortense's husband, was no longer avoided, and Hortense began to talk about good memories and Immy's dear, dead, sainted father. Their lives went on.

Twenty-Two

"There's not much I can do," Stinton Ogilvie Braden said to Immy after he'd been in to see Hortense. "I'm not a criminal lawyer." From the looks of his suit, he was a successful one, though.

"Well, you're our only family lawyer. Can't you help her?" Immy didn't like the way Tabitha was cocking her head toward them, pretending she was doing paperwork. "We need to talk somewhere private."

They left the lobby and got into his Lexus. "This is better," said Immy. "So, we need a criminal lawyer? There are criminal charges?"

"I've already called a colleague who should be here shortly," said Mr. Braden. He was a long, lanky man whose head nearly brushed the top of the car. His accompanying aroma, eau de tobacco, permeated the soft leather they sat on. "Woman by the name of Sarah Joyce."

"What's her last name?"

"Joyce. Her name is Sarah Joyce."

"OK." Immy supposed having two first names was better than having three last ones, like Mr. Braden. "How's Mother holding up?"

"She told me she's feeling hungry. I'll have Joyce bring a sandwich in to her. Is there a shop here where we can pick one up?"

"I can make one at home. It's closer and cheaper than the All Sips, and Mother just bought groceries. What's happening in there? Are they torturing her? Rubber hoses? Tasers?"

"Of course not, Imogene." He lit a cigarette but had mercy and rolled down his window.

"I guess not, at least while you're there."

"Your mother will not be tortured. She's sitting comfortably in a chair, and they are asking her questions. I've advised her not to answer any until her counsel arrives."

"She needs to come clean and tell them everything that happened. Unless … you don't think she killed Uncle Huey, do you?" There, she had said it.

"That's not my place."

"You do! You do think she killed him."

The lawyer twisted his thin frame around so he faced Immy. "To tell you the truth, I do not think she did, but what I think has no bearing on her case. I'm not going to represent her. From the little she told me, I rather think she has an idea you might have done it. The chief also thinks her initial lies about being in the vicinity were probably to protect you." He turned to face front and started the engine. Immy could barely hear the purr. "Shall we get your mother something to eat?"

Immy had had inklings that her mother might suspect her but hadn't put it together with Hortense's actions. So the lies all were to protect Immy? That did make sense. It also made sense that Hortense had murdered Huey, unfortunately.

They drove to the trailer, where Immy slapped together a baloney sandwich and grabbed a lunch-sized bag of chips. The chips were procured for Drew's lunches but were usually eaten by Hortense, since Drew wasn't crazy about chips.

Braden steered his black Lexus back to the station and pulled up beside its twin, only this one was silver. "Looks like Joyce is here," he said. Did all lawyers drive Lexi? Immy wondered. She also wondered if Lexi was the plural of Lexus.

A small, wiry black woman in a blue silk suit jumped out of her car as they approached, scurried over to them, and grabbed Immy's hand.

"Glad to meetcha. Sarah Joyce." Her voice was tiny, childish almost, to match her size. "And you're Imogene. We gotta situation here, huh?" She rubbed her hands together, returned to her own car and pulled her briefcase from the back seat, then darted to the police station door, holding it open for Immy.

Mr. Braden moved like a tortoise next to Ms. Joyce's hare, Immy thought. She hoped the woman was as efficient as she seemed. She had enough energy to get the job done, anyway.

Tabitha ushered the new lawyer behind her sacred door, and Mr. Braden said he had some business to go over with Immy. He patted the leather briefcase he had carried in from his car.

He answered her look of alarm with, "Civil business, not criminal."

"I don't understand. This is a criminal matter, isn't it? Isn't that what you said?"

"Yes, but, as you know, I was the attorney for your uncle, Mr. Hugh Duckworthy, in his business endeavors. I brought along a copy of his will, since I knew I'd be seeing you here."

"Uncle Huey's will? Why would I want that?"

"Perhaps because you're his principal beneficiary."

The front door opened, and Ralph walked in. "Hey, Immy. Just finished patrol." A huge grin lit his face. "Five more days."

"It's just dinner, Ralph."

"I know." His smile didn't dim a single watt.

Immy wasn't sure if this was an occasion that called for introducing people or not, so she erred on the side of politeness. "Ralph, this is the family lawyer, Mr. Braden."

The lawyer rose to his full height, which matched Ralph's, and they shook hands. Immy lost sight of Mr. Braden's thin hand in Ralph's paw. The two men may have been the same height, but it would have taken two Mr. Bradens to balance a Ralph on a scale.

"Ralph Sandoval, police officer for Saltlick," said Ralph. "Are you here for Mrs. Duckworthy?"

"Not exactly. Another attorney has been engaged for her. Do you mind if we carry out a civil transaction here? I need a witness's signature, too, so maybe you could provide that, if you have a moment."

"Sure," said Ralph. He shoved a chair next to Immy's and dropped into it.

Mr. Braden opened his briefcase and drew a sheaf of papers from it. "I'll need your signature here, Immy, and your initials here and here." He handed Immy the papers and his heavy gold pen, then flipped pages as she signed.

"If you would be so kind," he said to Ralph, who obediently inked his signature on the witness line on the last page.

When the signing was complete, the lawyer shuffled the paper a bit and handed Immy some of the pages. "This is your copy," he said.

"But what does this mean? I haven't read it." She opened her purse to stick the pages in. She intended to read them later. They looked too long to read here. "I inherit something?"

"The main provision states that you inherit the business. You are the new owner of Huey's Hash. There is no stipulation …"

Immy jumped to her feet. "What? I own the restaurant?" Her purse tumbled to the floor, spilling its contents. "I don't want the restaurant." She couldn't own the place. She didn't even work there anymore, and she was glad about that.

Ralph knelt down and started scooping up Immy's things.

"You don't have to keep it," the lawyer said. "If you'd like to put it on the market, I can …"

"Holy shit." Ralph's voice was soft. He slowly raised his eyes to Immy's. "Holy damn shit."

Immy had no idea what his problem was. Ralph held a wad of bills in his hand, some of the money Baxter had given her. Could he tell it had come from Baxter? Why should that upset him so?

Ralph stood. His voice assumed a deep, steely authority she had never before heard in it. "Stay right there." He turned to Tabitha. "Get the chief. Now."

Immy sank to the hard plastic chair. "What is it, Ralph? What's wrong?"

She felt a cold snake of fear slithering up her spine. What had she done?

"BUT I DIDN'T STEAL ANYTHING," Immy said for the third, maybe the fourth, time. She had lost track.

"Let's start at the beginning one more time." The chief's voice was getting weary but not as weary as Immy's. Her mouth was dry, and she felt slightly dizzy. The ceiling fan, barely stirring the stale air in the interrogation room, had the most annoying buzz.

When Ralph handed her money to the chief and fanned it out, she had seen that there were checks stuck in between some of the bills, but she had no idea where they came from or who they were made out to. They must have been in the money when Baxter gave it to her.

"I was at the park, having a picnic with my daughter, Nancy Drew Duckworthy." Immy was careful to speak into the mike.

"You don't have to repeat her full name every time, Immy," said Chief.

Ms. Joyce piped up. "She's following your instructions, sir. She's relating everything from the beginning."

Hortense had been released when Immy had been brought back for questioning. After a quick consultation in which Immy couldn't tell the lawyer anything because she had no idea why she was being questioned, Ms. Joyce had said she would sit in on Immy's session. It was comforting to have the little bulldog of a woman beside her.

"Go on," said Chief with a sigh.

"OK, so Baxter Killroy saw us at the park, and he pushed Drew for a while in the swing. She loves swings. Then Drew saw a friend from her preschool and she …"

Immy noticed the chief's eyes were closing. "OK, so I told Baxter about my fine for the fire damage. The five hundred dollars? And he said he'd like to help me out."

"What was the reason for this unbelievable offer?" asked Chief. "What did he expect in return?"

Immy hadn't been completely honest about this yet but decided maybe she should fess up. "Can I speak with my attorney? A sidebar?" Maybe if she told all, the snaky feeling in her spine and the pool of liquid acid roiling her stomach would both go away.

"A sidebar is something you do in court," said Ms. Joyce. She shot the chief a belligerent look, and he eased out of his chair and left the room.

"So, is the room bugged?" said Immy.

"Probably not, but we can go outside, if you'd rather."

Ralph was assigned to keep an eye on them while they paced the sidewalk in front of the station. Ms. Joyce seemed incapable of standing still. It was mid-afternoon. No clouds hindered the sun, and the day was turning warm. Immy had to work to keep up with the small woman's movements.

"It was sort of blackmail," said Immy. She told the lawyer about her and Baxter agreeing not to say either of them had been at the motel in Cowtail for the drug bust, but then it became known that she and her family were there, so he had no hold on her.

"Sounds more like a bribe."

Immy realized she had better brush up on her technical terms.

"They probably know Killroy was there, too," said Ms. Joyce. "He's on the verge of being charged with drug manufacturing. I know the guy representing Killroy's partner, the one they picked up in Cowtail the day of the fire. Good job exposing them, by the way." Joyce's smile was quick and bright.

"Omigod. He paid me the five hundred to keep it quiet that he was there. I wonder if he thinks I sang." The snakes slithered inside her.

"Sang what?"

"Turned stool pigeon. Ratted him out. Are you all right?"

Ms. Joyce appeared to have indigestion. "It's your terminology. Bothers my stomach."

Immy hoped the lawyer wasn't ignorant of legal terms.

"So the money with the incriminating checks came directly from Killroy," said Ms. Joyce. "He most likely stole it, but they can't put him in the restaurant for the murder. I called his attorney on the way here, and he told me Killroy admits being there the next morning and robbing the place, but he says he only took the charity box by the cash register, the money earmarked for United Way. Killroy says he didn't open the cash drawer."

"We never had that much in the charity box. Isn't it possible he's lying?"

"Of course. He almost certainly is, and that'll be our angle."

They returned to the still, airless room, and Ms. Joyce argued the position with Chief. Immy worked on not throwing up.

"Let's summarize," said Chief, looking at the lawyer while he addressed Immy. "You're saying you got the money from Killroy, who stole it while he was in the restaurant the morning after Hugh's murder. Killroy says he stole some money, but not that money. That money started in the cash drawer, dammit, or at least the checks with it did. Those checks are made out to Huey's Hash on the day Hugh died. It was a Monday when he was murdered, and the bank says he made his deposit Saturday. That's your story? "

Ms. Joyce nodded. Immy couldn't manage to say anything. Her story? She was getting dizzier trying to figure out what would happen to her.

"We have you in the vicinity of a possible meth operation. I'm not convinced that was all innocent."

Immy whimpered.

"We also have you in possession of stolen property from a murder scene, and I don't believe much of what you're telling about that either. Frankly, this all seems tied together, and we have a murder to solve."

Immy's feeling were hurt. "Can't you get the killer's fingerprints from the money?"

"There will only be about eight thousand fingerprints all over the damn money." Chief slapped the table, and Immy jumped. Even Ms. Joyce flinched. "I'm going to untangle this mess and find out what happened if it takes a year."

He threw the door opened and yelled for Ralph. "Lock her up," he roared.

The little lawyer planted herself in front of the chief. "On what grounds are you holding her?"

"Engaging in organized criminal activity. Money laundering in connection with a felony offense. Abetting drug fraud. But mostly, failure to identify. Need some more?" The chief sidestepped Ms. Joyce and stormed off toward his office at the back of the building while Ralph led Immy across the hall. She considered resisting but knew Ralph could pick her up and carry her to a cell if he wanted to.

Chief turned outside his office door. "Ralph, get Killroy in here and lock him up. Hortense, too. We'll get to the bottom of this."

"You can't do that!" Joyce squeaked after him.

"Watch me," he flung over his shoulder just before he slammed his door.

Ralph solemnly read Immy her rights and took her fingerprints, then ushered her into a small cell. "I'm really sorry, Immy." He looked on the verge of tears as he swung the cell door closed and locked it.

"That's all right, Ralph," she said. "Not your fault. I didn't know those checks were in the money. If I knew, wouldn't I take them out and get rid of them?"

She could hear Ms. Joyce yelling in the hallway. "You'll hear from me. You'll release her or else."

"Why am I locked up, Ralph?"

"You heard Chief. Organized crime, money laundering, and failure to identify. As a witness, I'm sure. "

Damn, Immy wished she had a reference book with her. What the hell was failure to identify?

Twenty-Three

Immy plopped onto the lower cot. It was almost as hard as the chairs in the lobby, but it seemed softer than the chair she had been in for the last three hours. It was going to be a challenge to solve Hugh's murder, locked up like this. And, dammit, they were bringing Mother in, too.

Drew! Who would take care of Drew? The snake inside her hardened and turned to resolve. She had issues to take care of.

"I demand my one phone call," yelled Immy, trying to rattle the bars of her cage. They were solidly attached and made no noise, wouldn't even wobble, so she shouted louder. "You have to give me my one phone call."

Ralph came running. "Who do you want to call, Immy? Everyone knows you're here, and you just saw that lawyer."

"Oh, good, you haven't left yet. I have to make arrangements for Drew."

She visualized the insides of Ralph's head spinning slowly while he thought about this. Evidently, he decided it would be a good idea. "OK," said Ralph. "I'll bring you a cell phone."

She glanced at the time on the borrowed phone before she called Clem at the diner. It was almost four. She hoped Mother would get to eat a snack before they locked her up. She didn't want to imagine what dinner would be like in here. Maybe that little lawyer woman would spring them before long.

"Hi, Clem. I have a favor to ask." She thought he sounded harried. "How's the business going?" With a jolt, Immy realized that the business was now her business. She owned it. She wondered if the money and the checks from the cash drawer would ever make it back to the business. An owner would have to think of things like that. The bottom line, Huey always said. That was the most important thing.

"Couldn't be busier," Clem said. "The more trouble you cause, young lady, the better it is for this place." Did he chuckle? Did he think her predicament was funny?

If his reasoning held water, there ought to be a line around the block when word of her arrest got out, but she didn't want word to get out. She didn't belong here.

"Clem, don't tell anyone, but I'm in the big house." Immy wondered how many filthy perps had breathed into this phone. It smelled like years of bad breath. She moved it a half inch away from her mouth.

"Whose house is it, that new one on the edge of town? I wondered who was building it."

"I'm in jail!"

"What did you do?"

"Nothing! They're all trumped up charges."

"What are the trumped up charges?" She heard a clatter in the background. "Baxter," shouted Clem, trying to muffle the phone with his hand. "If you break one more glass, you're fired." He returned his attention to Immy. "At least he's not in jail."

But he soon would be, Immy knew, as soon as Ralph rounded him up.

"Clem, Mother is going to be locked up, too."

"You ladies running a crime ring or something?"

"We haven't done anything! I told you, trumped up charges. Organized crime. Abetting something."

There was a brief lull, then Clem replied. "Abetting what?"

Good question. "Something to do with Uncle Huey's murder, I guess. Or maybe the robbery, if they're separate. And maybe something about drugs. I'm not sure, but could you run over and get Drew? She'll be alone after they take Mother in."

"Don't worry, sweetie." His volume rose. "Baxter, mind the store for a few minutes. I have to pick up Drew."

"Wait. Don't have Baxter do it."

"Why not?"

"He's about to be arrested, too."

A longer lull this time. "You must be running a crime ring. Are they rounding up the whole town? I need a busboy here, Immy. The other worthless bum didn't show up, and after I gave him a whole week off. It's almost supper time. I can't really afford to run to your house."

Immy looked at Ralph, loitering outside her cell, waiting to take the phone away when she finished. "Wait a sec, Clem." She held the phone away from her mouth. "Ralph, could you drop Drew at the diner when you pick Mother up?"

He pushed off the wall and walked to her bars. "I guess so. I don't see why not. I have to go there to bring in Killroy anyway."

She told Clem to expect Ralph to drop Drew off and to expect to lose Baxter, no matter how much he needed him right now.

"One more thing, Clem. Are you taking extra precautions?" She didn't know if he'd gotten the anonymous note she had left for him, warning him of the contract job by Frankie's Uncle Guido.

"I always take extra precautions, Immy. Cook all the meat through and through."

She couldn't think of another way to ask him without revealing she had broken into his house when he wasn't there. Besides, Guido was a small man, and Clem probably weighed three times what he did. Maybe Clem could sit on Guido when Guido tried to off him.

The thought occurred to her that she was maybe involved in organized crime, if Chief was talking about Guido.

As UNCOMFORTABLE AS THE COT WAS, Immy must have fallen asleep, because she jolted upright when her cell door clanged open. If she had been half an inch taller, she would have bumped her head on the bottom of the top bunk.

"I'm so sorry, Hortense," said Ralph, sounding mournful. Mother stood in the doorway, dazed, looking like she was never going to take another step. Ralph gave her a gentle nudge, then another, but gentle nudges didn't have much effect on Hortense. He finally bent over, planted his hands on her back, and pushed her into the cell. The clang of the locking door had a cold, hollow sound. Immy jumped up, but Hortense staggered across the cell to the lower bunk. It sagged and groaned as she lowered her bulk onto it.

When Immy looked away, Baxter stood outside the bars, his hands cuffed behind his back. The look he shot Immy burned with hatred.

"Baxter," Immy said. "It's not my fault you're here."

"Then whose fault is it?"

"Move it, Killroy," said Ralph, no mourning in his voice now. "Over here." He grabbed Baxter's arm and pulled him.

Immy called after them as Ralph led Baxter out of sight to the adjoining cell. Saltlick only had three cells total. "I never ratted on you. Never. If they tell you I did, they're lying. The cops always lie to get you to confess, remember that."

Baxter's door banged shut, Ralph left without meeting Immy's eyes, and the felons were left alone.

Immy stood at the bars, trying to see Baxter, but she couldn't. Behind her, Hortense broke into a mournful wail. Was any of this Immy's fault? She sat beside Mother on the cot and patted her nice, round knee, then leaned her head onto Mother's soft shoulder. The shoulder gradually stopped quaking, and Hortense raised a hand to stroke her daughter's hair.

"You're a good girl, Immy," she whispered, her voice husky with crying.

Immy tried to accept the spirit of Mother's words. On the one hand, Mother wasn't blaming her for the mess they were in. She loved her for that. But she couldn't keep her other thoughts away. *I'm not a girl. I'm a woman, and I'll get us out of this.*

Her mind wandered to the next cell. She could hear low conversation. Was someone else in Baxter's cell? The hostility in Baxter's eyes had scared her, she had to admit. She needed to make sure he knew she hadn't put him here.

Giving her mother's knee one last pat, she walked to the front of the cell and pressed her forehead to the bars, getting herself as close to Baxter's cell as she could.

"Psst! Baxter."

"Leave me alone, Immy."

"Are you all right?"

"No, Immy, I am not all right. I'm in jail."

"I want you to know I didn't tell them anything."

No answer.

"I'm not the reason you're here."

"And how do you figure that?" He still didn't sound friendly, like he usually did. She needed to be more specific.

"I never told anyone you were at the motel. They didn't get that from me."

"That's not the main reason I'm here, Immy."

She heard shuffling in his cell. The next time he spoke, his voice was nearer. He must have gone to the bars at the front of his cell, too. "But I am here because of you."

"No, I never said anything bad about you."

"No, you just told them the money came from me."

"Because it did!"

Baxter's intake of breath sounded shaky. "Now they think I stole it. From there it's not a huge leap to murdering Hugh. You planted those checks in there to make them think I took that money from the till."

Immy jerked her head back from the bars. "I most certainly did not, but someone did." She slumped against the wall. Dust motes swirled in the sunbeams of the dying day, coming through the high, barred window. It was amazing there was dust in a place with such hard surfaces.

"Imogene, don't bite your lower lip like that," said Mother.

Immy leaned toward Baxter's cell again. The bars were still warm from her previous contact. "Baxter, where did you get that money? You said you didn't steal it, right?"

Silence.

"Is someone in that cell with you?" Maybe he didn't want to spill his guts with a potential stool pigeon so close.

"No, but Phil is in the next cell."

"Who's Phil?"

"He's the guy who was picked up at the motel."

"Oh, the one making meth in your room that you didn't know about." She heard a snigger from down the hall. "Did Phil give you that money?" Could Baxter have known about the meth lab? Come to think of it, how could he have not known? It was such stinky stuff. Was that the organized crime?

"Huh? No, it's none of your business where I got it."

"It most certainly is! That money is the reason we're all in jail, you idiot."

"And you didn't frame me with it? You sure about that?" said Baxter.

"Why on earth would I do that?"

"Immy, I don't know why the hell you do anything."

Immy took a moment to think. Whoever took that money might not have noticed the checks in it. She didn't, and Baxter didn't. On the other hand, they or he or she might have noticed the checks, might even have put them there. In which case, both she and Baxter were being framed — maybe by the killer.

"Look, Baxter. Those checks came from Huey's cash drawer. So the money probably came from there, too. If you didn't steal it, someone else did, maybe the killer."

"Probably the killer, babe. I think you're right." He sounded a little more friendly now, at least. Not so scary.

"OK, then. Who did you get the money from?"

"I came across it."

"Nobody's going to believe that."

"Tell me about it, but really, that's what happened."

"I believe you." *If it'll make you tell me where you got the money.* This could be a serious clue. It had to be.

"I don't know if you know that I quit bussing at the diner after Hugh got killed. Told Clem I quit. But then Clem called me in Saturday to rehire me. I said OK because my other venture hadn't quite worked out." Immy thought she heard that snigger again, and did another one come from Mother? "When I came out after talking to Clem that morning, there was a paper bag on the ground next to my truck. All this money was in it."

Immy leaned her back against the wall and studied the ceiling, considering Baxter's tale. "You didn't wonder where it came from?"

Hortense lifted her head. Immy could see the wheels in her mind turning as Mother narrowed her eyes and bit her own lower lip.

"Hey, money's money, but yeah, I did think it might be stolen. Guess I didn't think it would still be there, right outside the back door, if it was the money from the diner, though. That was Saturday I found it. Hugh was killed the Tuesday before that, right?"

"Monday night. You found him Tuesday."

"Yeah, you're right."

Immy drummed her fingers on one of the bars. "So where does that leave us?"

"In jail," said Baxter.

"Yes," agreed Hortense, "in jail."

Twenty-Four

Immy needed to find out who originally took the money, but how? It would probably have hundreds of fingerprints on it, as the chief had said. With red-rimmed eyes and raised brows, Mother was beckoning her over to the cot. Immy sat beside her again. Hortense lowered her voice to the tiniest whisper, which made it hard to hear her.

"You don't believe him, do you?" Mother asked.

"Why would I not believe him?"

"No one just finds a sack of money on the ground."

"I'm sure some people do, Mother." Surely, in the history of the world, people had found sacks of money on the ground. Why not Baxter?

"I wouldn't believe anything Baxter tells you. He is not to be trusted."

Immy remembered the chief telling her to be careful around him, Ralph telling her the same thing, and now her mother telling her not to trust him. Should she persist in believing him in the face of all these negative people? Maybe not, but then again …

"Mother, if Baxter did steal that money, wouldn't he have thrown the checks away?"

"Unless he was attempting to frame you."

"But he should know I would tell someone where I got the goods when I got caught red-handed, although I wouldn't have gotten caught if my purse hadn't dumped on the floor in the police station."

"I can hear you, you know," came from the next cell.

Immy realized their voices had gradually risen. "Sorry, Baxter."

"But you're right," he said. "If we knew who put the money there by my truck, we could shift the blame and get outta here."

"Was the sack made of paper?" asked Mother.

"Yeah," said Baxter.

It was weird talking to Baxter but not being able to see him. It was like he was disembodied, a ghost or something.

"Then it might have retained fingerprints," Hortense said.

"Mother, you're thinking like a detective." Immy herself heard the pride ring in her statement. Hortense rolled her eyes.

A loud, whanging noise startled Immy and Hortense. "Damn," said Baxter. "I threw that fuckin' bag away, and I think I just broke my fuckin' hand whackin' this fuckin' bar."

"Language," said Hortense.

There was probably no possibility of retrieving the bag. Baxter said he'd stuffed it into the dumpster behind the restaurant. Immy knew how full the dumpster had been Thursday when she had fallen into it. Baxter added the sack on Saturday, and the bin wouldn't be emptied until Tuesday, which was tomorrow.

"I don't suppose there's any possibility the sack could be retrieved from the detritus?" said Mother.

Immy jumped off the cot. "Cops are always going through garbage for clues, Mother. Of course they can do it. Ralph!"

RALPH WAS EAGER TO TRY TO RETRIEVE the sack, and Chief Emersen thought it was worth a try, too.

Later that night, though, when Ralph returned from his mission, his attitude seemed to have changed. He'd been gone for hours, and Immy couldn't help but notice it had started to pour while he was gone. She pictured him in the dumpster, getting wet. Surely, though, there was a nifty tent or canopy or something the cops erected over dumpsters when they searched them in the rain.

Ralph stormed through the heavy metal door and stood before Immy and Hortense's cell. Rivulets ran from his clothing onto the concrete floor and dripped from his black hair.

"Do you know what-all is in a dumpster like that?"

Immy had never seen him so mad. Or so wet. Or smelling so bad.

"Do you?"

Immy started to answer his question, as she knew only too well what was there. "There are definitely coffee grounds, and leftovers from people's plates, and sauce, and ..."

"So you do know, and you sent me there anyway."

Hortense cleared her throat. "I believe your superior officer is the one who dispatched you on that errand."

Ralph transferred his glare from Immy to her mother. He lifted a shoe, which made a sucking sound. "Some idiot dumped a pile of sugar right outside the station door. I stepped in damn melted sugar coming in." He shook his shoe, and a scrap of pink paper floated to the floor.

"So," said Immy, wondering if it was wise to prolong discussion of the dumpster, "y'all don't have a tent thing to cover you up when you're dumpster diving?"

"We do not have a tent thing, no. We certainly do not."

Baxter's voice rang from the next cell. "Ralphie! Did you find the freakin' sack?"

The glance Ralph threw in his direction was sharp. So was his answer. "Yes, and since it was so deep, it didn't get soaked by the rain. Like I did." He spun and exited through the metal door again.

"That boy needs a shower," said Hortense.

Immy agreed.

THE NEXT MORNING, TUESDAY, DAWNED clear and bright. And early, since there were no curtains on the cell windows. Immy was beginning to panic about her PI job. She was supposed to show up on Wednesday. What would she say if she couldn't make it because she was in jail?

Before breakfast could be served, the chief came to their cell and told Immy and Hortense that their lawyer had posted bail for them. She had convinced everyone they weren't flight risks before the next grand jury sitting, Chief said. Immy would have kissed the little woman if she had been there at the moment.

The snick of the door being unlocked was the sweetest sound Immy had heard since she said goodbye to Drew yesterday. Drew's voice was always the very sweetest thing in Immy's life.

"Hey, Chief," said Baxter from his cell. "What about me? I need to see a doctor. My hand hurts like hell."

"I haven't seen your lawyer, Killroy."

"I ain't got one. You gonna get me one?"

"We're working on it, son," said the chief.

Immy wondered if that was the truth.

"We'll get someone to look at your hand today."

To her surprise, her mother threw her arms around Chief Emersen. "Thank you, thank you, thank you, Emmett. I couldn't have borne to eat another ghastly repast in this place. There was nothing prandial about that meal last night." Hortense fell short of kissing the chief, but her hug went on for a while. Eventually, the chief peeled her arms off him and led them out through the metal door.

Immy looked back on the cell. She was elated to be on this side of the bars. It was without a doubt the worst place she had ever spent a night. Following the chief and her mother down the hall, she realized Mother was probably even riper smelling than she herself was, and she could sure smell herself.

Baxter called out as they exited through the metal door, but Immy couldn't understand his words, lost in the clanging, just that he was angry. That was probably because they were leaving and he wasn't, but she couldn't help that. She hoped she would never see those bars from the inside again.

The tiny lawyer, Sarah Joyce, waited in the lobby. Immy ran to her and threw her arms around the woman's thin shoulders. To her dismay, tears started to flow. She backed off, embarrassed, and smoothed the green silk of Ms. Joyce's jacket where she had rumpled it.

"Sorry," Immy mumbled. "We're so grateful you got us out of there."

Hortense, maintaining her dignity, but with a definite tremor in her topmost chin, shook Ms. Joyce's hand. "Our gratitude knows no bounds, Ms. Joyce. Please accept our humble appreciation and our undying …"

"Do you girls need a ride home?" The lawyer cut Hortense's effusiveness short, and Immy silently thanked her. Luckily, their release was in time for her job tomorrow. The PI, Mike Mallett, had called it a job interview, but she was pretty sure she would be hired. After all, had the other applicants, assuming there were any, read *The Moron's Compleat PI Guidebook* cover to cover?

"We'll need to get my daughter," said Immy.

"Where is she?" asked Ms. Joyce.

"What time is it?" Immy glanced at the wall clock above Tabitha's glass fortress. It was just after eight in the morning. "I guess she'll be at Huey's Hash with Clem."

"To Huey's Hash, then." The tiny woman scurried through the front door and held it while Hortense lumbered out and Immy followed.

Ms. Joyce opened the two right side doors of her silver Lexus and whisked herself around to the driver's side. Immy closed the front door after Hortense climbed in. Immy wanted more than anything to see Drew again. It would be something normal, something not related to jail or to Uncle Huey's murder or to Baxter. She had no desire to examine her feelings about Baxter any time soon. A thought hit her as she bent down to get into the back seat. She straightened.

"Wait a minute," she said to the women in the front seat. "I have to tell Ralph something." She returned to the lobby. Ralph had been standing and watching them depart. He brightened when she walked over to him.

"Ralph," Immy said, "I think I know of another suspect you could finger for Huey's murder, someone who might have offed him."

"Besides you and Hortense and Xenia and Frankie and Baxter?"

"Well, yes."

Ralph waited. Was he using the silence trick to make her spill her guts? No matter, she was going to spill them anyway.

"Yes. I overheard a conversation I wasn't supposed to in the hospital parking garage when I went there to interrogate Xenia."

"When did you do that?"

"When she was unconscious."

"How did that go?"

Immy took a breath. "I didn't succeed in questioning her that time, but let me tell you what I heard Frankie say to his Uncle Guido in the parking lot."

Ralph's brown eyes narrowed. He gave her more of the silent treatment.

"I think Frankie was asking his Uncle Guido to do a hit on Clem. I mean, at first I thought Frankie was asking him to do Uncle Huey, but he was already dead. Then I figured out Frankie thought Clem was responsible for Xenia's accident. I mean, I had just told Frankie that Huey was dead. So Frankie must have been taking out a contract on Clem with his Uncle Guido."

"Huh?"

She could kick Ralph in the shins when he said huh like that, not that it would probably hurt him.

"I said, Frankie must have been taking out …"

"I know what you said, but what does that have to do with anything?" Ralph scratched his head, making his coarse, dark hair spike oddly. "Oh, I guess if Clem turns up murdered, we'll know who to …"

"I suspect Guido murdered Huey, too."

"Why do you think that?"

"Don't you see? Guido is a hit man. Hit men kill people. He probably killed Huey. No one else seems to be guilty."

Ralph looked down and shuffled his large feet. "That's not true. Everyone seems to be guilty."

Did he mean she seemed to be guilty? Immy puffed her breath out at the obtuse Ralph. "Are you going to question Guido or not?"

"I'll run it by Chief. He has to decide."

Immy thought she knew what Chief would decide. Her shoulders sagged, and she walked outside.

A colorful display caught the corner of her eye on the way to Ms. Joyce's car. On the wall beside the door, letters were spelled out. Pink saccharin packets, stuck to the wall, spelled out HOR. Beneath that, yellow Splenda packets formed the letters OT. And below them, blue Equal packets wrote GUILTY. They seemed to be glued to the bricks.

She ran back inside the lobby. "Ralph, did you not see that sign outside?"

He followed her out, and she pointed to the message.

"Well, I'll be damned."

"It's a clue, Ralph."

"It's a bunch more sugar packets. The ones last night were all white, real sugar. These are all fake sugar."

"Read it, Ralph."

He squinted and read them. "Ho ot guilty."

"Hor, not Ho." But Immy looked again. The pink packets that had made a letter R had fallen to the ground since she had first spied the message. Other pink packets lay scattered beneath the message along with a few yellow ones. What had it originally spelled, Immy wondered.

"So, whores are hot and guilty? Is that what it's saying?"

Immy frowned. "I'm not sure."

IMMY SAT IN HER BEDROOM AFTER breakfast and played Barbies with Drew for about half an hour. She had decided not to send Drew to school today. Immy didn't want to let her out of her sight for a while for a reason she couldn't explain.

Immy also stewed over what to do about Guido. Maybe she had talk to the chief herself. Maybe when she started her new job tomorrow, she would gain more credibility as an investigator. She wondered if she would carry some sort of a license. Maybe she would have to take a test to become a PI. Then her thoughts stretched to arriving at Mr. Mallett's office in the morning. She would stride in with purpose in her step so he'd see she was someone who could get the job done. Wait a minute. What would she be wearing?

"I'll be right back, sweetie." Immy set Ken on the floor and hurried to the living room. "Mother," she started.

"Imogene, can I not watch a daytime drama in peace? You are aware that I missed all of my shows yesterday?"

"Yeah, no TV in the hoosegow."

Drew had followed Immy. "No TV in the hoosegow?" she echoed.

Hortense raised the volume on the set.

"I'm going into Wymee Falls." Immy raised her voice to match that of the gleeful game show contestant. "I need a suit for my job tomorrow."

Hortense muted the television, which had switched to a commercial, and eyed her daughter. "I suppose it would be advantageous to make a favorable sartorial impression at your interview."

"Yes, it would. Drew, want to go for a ride?"

Immy let Drew take two Barbies in the van, and they had a pleasant drive into town.

"Did you have a good time at Uncle Clem's?" Immy asked, tossing her words to the backseat where Drew sat in her car seat.

She saw Drew shrug in the rearview mirror.

"I thought he bought you new Barbies and played with you."

"Yeah, he did, but I missed you, Mommy." Drew's big green eyes bored into Immy's heart.

"We won't do that again, sweetie. We won't leave you anywhere."

"What if you go back to the jailhouse?"

Yeah, what if?

"Unca Clem was sad," said Drew.

Immy threw a glance over her shoulder at her daughter. "Sad about what?"

"He was so sad. He cry-ed. He was sad Geemaw was in the jailhouse. He said he was gonna get her outta there."

Immy laughed. "I wonder how he thought he was going to do that. I didn't notice him posting any bail."

"I helped him."

"That was a good girl. I'm glad you helped."

"Look, Mommy, the waterfall is going!"

Sure enough, the waterfall had been turned on. The pump usually stayed turned off until the spring rains.

"Tell me the waterfall story again, Mommy," said Drew, ducking her head to get a better look at the cascade.

Immy slowed so Drew could see it longer.

"OK. Once upon a time there was a real waterfall, back when Indians roamed the high plains surrounding the narrow Wymee River." The so-called river ranged from a trickle to a good-sized stream, depending on the time of year. "It must have been an awfully small waterfall, though, because it disappeared mysteriously when the settlers started to come. They had already called the place …"

"Wymee Falls," chirped Drew, supplying this bit of the narrative by family tradition.

"So the town fathers and some mothers decided to build themselves a waterfall beside the river. Now we have a pump to carry the water to the top of the man-made rock hill right beside the river. The water goes down, into the pool, and back up with the pump."

"Up and down, up and down." Drew ended the story.

Once again, Immy thought the waterfall might be a metaphor for her life.

She snagged a parking spot next to the mall entrance and she, Drew, and the Barbies trooped into the overly air conditioned enclosure to look for a suit Immy could afford. She was pretty sure a female PI should wear a suit.

They emerged victorious two hours later, stuffed full of fries and shakes, Immy carrying the new suit on a hanger and toting a bag with new shoes, purse, and a pair of pantyhose. Drew proudly waved a new Ken to passersby on the way to the van. Immy's purse was noticeably lighter, but that would be remedied soon.

Twenty-Five

They sat around the kitchen table to eat their Spaghetti-Os that night. Hortense had suggested it and turned the television off herself. This was how Immy had always imagined a real family eating supper, around a table, with no television.

"Imogene, there is a meeting of the librarians association tomorrow in Wymee Falls."

"Do you need a ride?"

"No, no, I'm getting picked up, but Drew will need to be tended to."

"I'll drop her off at school on my way to work," offered Immy.

Hortense gave Immy a doubtful look. "On the way to your job interview? You haven't yet told me specifically what this job will entail."

"Oh, it's a little of this and a little of that, I think. I'll know more later today."

"I had a job," said Drew. "I helped Unca Clem, Geemaw." Immy beamed at her daughter, making dinner conversation along with the grownups.

"That's nice, dear," her grandmother answered.

"He juss about ran out of sugar."

Sugar? Clem? Immy froze for a moment. "What do you mean?" asked Immy.

Drew pulled back at the sharpness in her tone. Immy softened it, paused a moment, and spoke sweetly.

"What exactly was Uncle Clem doing when you helped him?"

"It was so fun." Drew put her spoon down so her hands could help her describe the experience. "We got alllll the sugar," her arms made a big circle, "and it was late and dark outside, and I got to stay up really, really late." She flapped her hands at the thought of the joyful experience. "And we put the sugar at the pleece station. That's where the jailhouse is, Unca Clem said."

Drew picked up her spoon and scooped little noodle Os into her mouth, then added to her tale before Immy could collect herself enough to comment.

"And then we went out early, early, and Unca Clem took my schoo' glue and put some more clues because he said," Drew paused to breathe, "he said the rain came and ruint the other sugars and now he was gonna put colored ones out and not put them onna ground so they wouldn't melt."

Her dissertation done, she returned her attention to her bowl.

Immy and Hortense stared at each other.

"Drew, dear," said Hortense "what was Uncle Clem's reason for these bizarre actions?"

"He said he was gonna save you."

Immy pictured the message she had seen: HOR OT GUILTY, with a pile of pink packets that had fallen off the wall. If Clem had used school glue, the morning dew may have loosened his handiwork soon after he'd done it. There were enough blue packets for an N. Had the message said HORTENSE NOT GUILTY? What on earth did Clem think that would accomplish? Maybe he'd taken heed of the anonymous note she had left him and decided anonymous messages were a good way of communicating. Immy was about to decide that maybe they weren't. None of them seemed to have any effect, except the phone call she had left about Frankie's cigarette butt in the diner. But Frankie had been questioned, released, and had now disappeared.

"Mother," said Immy. "Do you think we should tell Chief Emersen, or maybe Ralph, that Clem is the one who left those packets glued to the station wall?"

Hortense sighed, thinking. "What would that accomplish? The dear man is merely trying in his misguided way to divert suspicion from me."

"Well, maybe he knows something. Maybe he's sitting on some clues. He's acting strangely."

"He is intoxicated, Imogene. The poor man is drunk on love, that's all it is. I believe, with my greater accumulation of years, that I am a somewhat better judge of character than yourself."

Immy closed her eyes, then opened them quickly. Thoughts of her mother and Clem sometimes produced pictures in her head that she would rather not see.

WEDNESDAY MORNING WAS OVERCAST, the air heavy with impending rain. Immy donned her new work clothes, a soft green suit over an old sleeveless shell that was only stained at the hem in the back. The new shoes, fake alligator, looked great. They weren't exactly the right size, but they'd been on sale, and she was sure she could wear them for a few hours.

She dropped Drew off and headed out of Saltlick. On the drive into Wymee Falls for her ten o'clock interview, she tried to figure out what to do about Clem. He had the looks of a jolly Saint Nick, but all her life she had never gotten a warm feeling toward him, like her mother apparently did. Maybe that was because Immy had worked with him and knew what an explosive temper lurked behind his ruddy jowls. She had always partly attributed that to his profession. Didn't all cooks have temper tantrums? They worked in a heated environment and were under pressure to get the food out quickly and fill the orders correctly. They never heard praise from the diners unless the wait staff decided to pass compliments on to them, which the wait staff was often too rushed and stressed to do. Cooks got plenty of negative feedback when they saw plates half full of their handiwork come back and get scraped into the trash. And Clem could not be convinced that most people wanted less to eat than he did, so he insisted on serving huge portions, guaranteeing that half of almost every meal was not consumed. Sometimes customers took the leftovers home, but most didn't. Clem saw his golden chicken-fried steaks, now soggy, his creamy white gravy, now congealed, and his crisp sweet potato fries, now limp, all returned to the kitchen as trash. It must be disheartening, Immy thought.

Lightning bolts to the west startled her out of her thoughts.

Before she knew it, she was at the traffic light a block from Detective Mike Mallett's office. It didn't look like there were any parking spaces in front of his building. She had to park two blocks away, and her feet were beginning to ache from the stiff, too-short shoes by the time she reached the small wooden building crammed between two multi-story stone office buildings.

On her previous visit to the office, when she had pushed her resume under the door, she had thought the office cold and dark. Now, with storm clouds gathering overhead, the lighted window looked cheery and welcoming.

Immy paused at the door. His name was printed neatly: Mike Mallett, Private Investigations.

Did one knock? In PI novels people usually knocked on the door, but the office was usually in a rundown building, up several stories without a working elevator in a building with a dance studio or a couple of lawyers and a bail bondsman. Sometimes there was a bar on the ground floor. There wasn't a bar within blocks of Detective Mallett's office.

She decided just to open the door and walk in. After all, if he was advertising for help, he might not have a receptionist and could be in the back.

He wasn't.

A small, weasely looking guy sat at a gray metal desk. The desk, some unpadded folding chairs, and one file cabinet were the complete furnishings of the bare-walled anteroom. He rose when she walked in but not very far. He couldn't have been much taller than five feet. Immy wondered if his small size enabled him to blend in and be more invisible on surveillance projects.

"You must be Imogene Duckworthy." His voice was as raspy in person as it had been on the phone. He didn't look sick, so Immy thought it must be his normal voice. That rasp wouldn't blend in at all.

"Very pleased to meet you, Detective Mallett."

"Oh, please call me Mike," he said with a wave in her direction.

The room smelled of something, but Immy couldn't place it. Walnuts?

He walked around the desk, reached out a hand, and they shook. "C'mon back," he said, leading the way through a door to what was obviously his own office. It wasn't much more furnished than the outer office, but the chairs were padded. It also held a small, round table with two straight-backed chairs. Detective Mallett gestured Immy into one of these and shoved a pile of paper to the side of the table as he sat across from her.

Immy was disappointed he didn't wear a rumpled trench coat, but maybe he did when he went out. His white shirt looked rumpled, at least, and his gray tie was loosened and askew.

The walnut smell was a little stronger in this room. Immy spied a candle burning on the battered oak desk.

"What scent is that candle?" she asked, hoping to impress him with her powers of observation.

"I don't know, just somethin' to take out the nicotine reek. I quit the cancer stick habit again last week but fell off the wagon this morning."

Was he going to smoke in the office? Immy wasn't sure she would be able to work there if he did.

"Don't worry." He must have seen her thought in her face. "If I hire you, I won't smoke in here no more."

Immy gave him a half-smile. Should she believe him?

"Now, what makes you think you wanna work here?"

She told him that she had read *The Moron's Compleat PI Guidebook* cover to cover several times (twice was several, right?) and was part way through *Criminal Pursuits*.

"Yeah, yeah, but what makes you think you wanna work here?"

Immy took a deep breath. She had to answer questions? Was it possible he was not going to hire her? She blinked back her tears. "I've wanted nothing else my whole life but to work with a real detective." She stopped to breathe and try to take the tremor out of her voice. "My father was one, and it's my life's ambition." Of course, her life's ambition was to be a detective, not an assistant, but this was a first step. "Also, I'd like to buy my own car."

"What kinda hours can you put in?"

"Since I share a car and have a daughter who gets dropped off and picked up at daycare, I guess I'll have to work around her schedule."

"Can you do ten to two at least?"

"Oh, yes!" Now it sounded like he was going to hire her.

"How are you at office work? Any experience?"

Immy froze. "Office work?"

"Yeah, how are you on the computer?"

"Really good. I'm really good on the computer." Her family didn't own one, but she had used them in high school. She knew PIs had to use the computer to track down felons and look up arrest records. She would buy a *Compleat Guidebook* on computers today.

"Yeah? I could use a computer whiz. My typing is for shit."

Typing? "I can type." Not very quickly, but it's just pressing keys, right?

"Spreadsheets? You do spreadsheets? I need a better way to keep track of expenses and billing."

"I'm not sure. I think I can do that."

"I'm tempted to give you a try. The other gals that answered the ad, well one of 'em wore a nose ring and a lip stud, made me hurt to look at that metal in her face. The other one came in flip flops. I'm tellin' ya. At least you can dress for an interview."

He stood up. "I'll give you a call."

"You mean, I can't start today?"

"Hey, you wanna start today? Knock yourself out, kid. Imogene, right?"

"Just Immy, actually. That's what everyone calls me except my mother. And … just call me Immy." Damn, she was babbling. But she was hired!

"You wanna talk money?" He offered her a salary for a twenty-hour work week, four hours a day, five days a week, and she accepted it. It was a little less than she had hoped for, but maybe there would be a raise when he saw how eager she was.

He lifted the stack of papers on the table, carried them to the outer office, and plopped them onto the bare metal desk. "You can start here. These all need filing. Knock yourself out."

She sat at her desk and surveyed her domain. Here she was, on her way to being a PI. At last!

With a clap that brought her halfway out of her secretary's chair, lightning struck somewhere close, and the dark clouds opened up outside. The office lights flickered but stayed on. Immy reached for her stack of papers and started through them, thinking it was rather pleasant watching the rain course down the picture window in front of her while she sat snug and secure, not to mention being paid.

After two hours of going through half the stack of miscellaneous papers, she felt like knocking herself out. Unconscious. She had succeeded in filing about one-fourth of the papers she had gone through. She had put the rest into another stack to ask for clarification on them later.

Some of the papers were strange. There were recipes ripped from magazines, and newspaper clippings about people who didn't have matching names on the files in the drawers behind her desk. Many were birth and death announcements. Some looked like copies of bills from Mallett Detective Agency, and some were receipts for office supplies. Those she knew what to do with. There were folders marked Income and Expense.

She had called home around eleven to tell her mother she was working today. Hortense hadn't been able to hide her astonishment.

"You're working? Where? At what?"

"In a PI's office." The moment of silence was satisfying. She could picture her mother's eyes bugging out, her mouth falling open. "Yep, a PI's office."

"I did hear you the first time. I wasn't questioning your statement. Maybe your sanity, Imogene. Are you sure about this?"

"Never surer, Mother." She gave her the address and phone number and got back to work.

It was now twelve-thirty, and she was cross-eyed from staring at papers. Should she ask about lunch? Should she have brought a sandwich? The food situation was very different, not working in a restaurant, the only other place she had ever worked.

Mike opened his door and laid a handwritten sheet of paper on the desk. "How you comin'? Ready for a break?"

Immy straightened her back and realized it was a little achy. "Sure."

"Quit doin' that for a while and type up these invoices for me, will ya?"

Oh. He meant a break from filing, not a break. "Sure," she said again with less enthusiasm. "Say, is there a lunch break?" She would never know if she didn't ask, and she didn't intend to skip lunch today. It would set a bad precedent.

"You wanna break, take one. If I'm ever gone and you wanna go out, just lock up. Oh, yeah, I better get you a key. Tell you what, you run out and bring us some eats. Looks like the rain stopped. I'll give you my key, and you can get a copy made while you're out. Deal?"

"Sure." This one was heartfelt. Errands would be welcome after all this paper handling.

IMMY LOCKED UP AND LEFT AT THREE, having put in four good, solid hours of work. She counted the errand running as work time, but not the lunch eating. She figured she was hired about 10:30 and took a half hour for lunch. Mike had left right after they ate sandwiches together at the round table in his office, saying he probably wouldn't be back today.

She had had a bad moment earlier when she began to wonder how to type up an invoice, but when she asked, Mike apologized for not showing her where the form was on the computer. It was easy to plug in the names and numbers from the sheet he'd scribbled them on, save them online, print them out, and mail them. Mike had taken the envelopes with him to drop at the post office when he left.

Unfortunately, her feet hurt so badly by quitting time, she had to walk barefoot the four blocks to her car. The space she had been in this morning, only two blocks away, had been taken when she returned from her lunch errands. The pavement was wet from the rain earlier, and her new pantyhose were ruined, but she was never going to wear those shoes again. Mike had said jeans and tees were OK in the office. She couldn't help but think the suit had gotten her the job, though.

Since she lacked the footwear necessary to enter a book store, she would have to get a *Moron's Compleat* computer book another day.

She sang to the radio on the way to get Drew. The rain started up again, but she had a job. She was almost a PI.

THAT EVENING RALPH CAME BY AFTER THEY'D EATEN. The family had reverted to eating in front of the television, since an old movie Hortense wanted to see was playing.

Immy opened the door and let him in.

"Hey, Immy, do you think …" he began.

Hortense cut him off with a withering look. "Do you think you could converse outside?"

"She can't hear when we talk," Immy whispered, pulling the door shut after their exit to the front porch. They sat on the wooden steps together. The stairs weren't quite wide enough for them to sit side by side without touching, as much room as Ralph took up. Almost, but not quite. The steps were only a little damp from the earlier storm.

"Mother missed her television when she was in jail. She's not being rude, just, well …" Mother was, of course, being rude.

The last streaks of a scarlet-hued sunset lingered in the west, throwing glints off the grass, still wet from the rain. The golden air carried the scent of honeysuckle from someone's yard.

"I wanted to tell you, that tip you gave us?" Ralph said.

"Um, which tip?" Had she given one that was not anonymous?

"You told me to have the chief check up on Frankie's Uncle Guido. Well, he did, and I brought him in today."

Oh, yes, that tip. What a relief. She wouldn't have to worry about Clem getting whacked now.

"Chief wants to bring Frankie in, too, but we can't find him."

"He's left town, right?"

"Looks like it. He hasn't been to his apartment since Saturday."

"Well, it's good Guido won't get at Clem anyway. Does it look like he killed Huey?"

"Nope. Doesn't look like he killed anyone here, in this country. He might have somewhere else, but Chief questioned him all afternoon before he let him go."

"He let him go?" So much for not worrying about Clem. She stared at Ralph. "Now he can kill Clem."

Ralph turned his head toward Immy. She thought he must have had onions for lunch. "I don't think he would kill someone when he's just been looked at by the police. That would be pretty stupid."

"But criminals are stupid. Everyone says so."

"Guido Giovanni doesn't strike me as a stupid guy."

"How does he strike you?"

"A lot smarter than that two-bit hood we do have locked up, Baxter Killroy. Oh, and I have some news you should hear about him, too."

His tone told Immy this was not going to be good news. A cricket serenade filled the brief silence.

"He's trying to make a deal to get out of the meth rap, and he's dancing around making some kind of admission for an old crime we've had him in mind for. If he doesn't admit it, we can't get him, but I wanted you to know about it. It concerns you."

The honeysuckle smelled stronger as the golden sunset glow faded and the darkness deepened. Immy waited for Ralph to gear up enough to tell her.

"Phil isn't a strong enough witness to stand up in court, and he could be shooting off his trap. But Phil says Killroy was the inside guy for the robbery ten years ago."

A chill running up Immy's spine sat her straight up. "The robbery? The one where my father was killed?"

"We're pretty sure Killroy didn't have anything to do with the killing, we've always thought that. We've also always suspected Killroy was the one who let them in, the two that did the killing. But he won't admit it, and we don't have any evidence other than a shaky hearsay."

Immy's shoulders caved in, and her insides sank to her soles. She had let that, that accomplice to murder kiss her. And more. She had made deals with him to protect him. She had been had.

Grabbing the railing, she pulled herself up and stumbled down the stairs, swallowing the bile that rose in her throat.

"You OK, Immy? Immy?" Ralph stood at the foot of the stairs, looking nervous and uncertain as Immy circled the small yard, pacing, putting her fury into each stomping step.

She stopped and looked up at Ralph Sandoval, standing there in his tired-looking uniform, his belly hanging over his belt just a bit, his coal-black hair looking messy in the twilight. He looked worried about her. "Are you on your way home from work, Ralph?"

He nodded. She knew he lived alone in a small trailer three blocks away. His parents had moved into Wymee Falls after his father retired from managing the video rental store and his sister had married a rancher and lived out near Amarillo, but she didn't know much more about him. He'd been two years ahead of her in school, so she figured he was two or three years older, but she didn't know if he had a cat or a dog, what movies he liked, or even what foods. He didn't have a quick wit, a sexy smile, or a tight rear like Baxter. But he was a solid gold person.

"Do you want to go to a movie Friday?" she asked. "I'm paying."

"Let's make it dinner and a movie." It looked like Ralph's face was turning a little pinkish, but it was hard to tell in the twilight.

She told Ralph about her job, and he seemed truly happy for her. She was glad someone approved of her career. They set a time for Friday, and Ralph left after saying goodbye and standing next to her awkwardly for about ten seconds before taking off.

Immy hoped the next time she saw Baxter Killroy he was dead.

Twenty-Six

Thursday after work, Immy picked up Drew, came home, and announced she wanted to take the family out.

Hortense muted the television and looked up. "Out? To eat?"

"Yes, to eat, Mother. Where would you like to go? You pick. I'll be getting a paycheck soon." Tomorrow, Immy was sure, since that would be Friday. People were supposed to get paid on Fridays. Not that Huey had ever paid on Fridays. In fact, he usually had to be reminded multiple times, but that was just Huey.

"Let me look." Hortense picked up the newspaper scattered on the floor next to her recliner. "I believe I spied a coupon for The Tomato Garden."

"You want to go there? That's the outfit that wanted to buy Huey's restaurant. Frankie Laramie's Uncle Guido owns the franchise."

"Yes, I'd like to inspect the establishment, never having dined on the premises. If they do still desire to purchase our family business, maybe we should delve further into the matter."

"Well, if you're sure." Immy didn't say that she knew it would be up to her, not up to her mother, if the restaurant were sold. But maybe she should consider selling to Guido, if he didn't turn out to be a murderer. Well, he probably was a murderer in the past when he was a hit man, but if he had killed Uncle Huey or if he eventually tried to kill Clem, she would definitely not sell to him. Could you even sell a restaurant to a person in prison? Immy had no idea. She didn't especially want to own it, though.

Hortense pushed her feet into her shoes and struggled to her feet.

"You want to go right now?" said Immy. "It's kind of early for supper."

"'Mato Garden, 'Mato Garden," sang Drew, jumping up and down. Her singsong vaguely resembled the jingle on the television ads. "Your fambly meets 'n' eats 'n' eats at 'Mato Garden, 'Mato Garden."

"It might be advantageous to arrive early, when they have fewer customers," said Hortense.

"OK. Wash hands, Drew, and we'll vamoose," said Immy, scrubbing her own at the kitchen sink.

The woman who greeted them at the door looked like a female version of Uncle Guido, small and dark. She even had a trace of his pencil mustache. Immy squinted to take a gander at the place in the dim lighting. Small candles tried to illuminate the round tables of laminated wood, all set with utensils wrapped in red and green cloth napkins. Overhead, tomato vines twined around dark wooden beams where dusty looking tomatoes drooped from their plastic stalks.

The part Immy liked was the tinkly, Italian-sounding music drifting from the speakers next to the ceiling.

"Three?" the mustachioed woman asked.

Hortense nodded, and they followed the woman to a table in the back, next to the kitchen door. Clatter from behind the door drowned out the soft accordions. Hortense gave the woman a pained expression. "Please. Your dining establishment is virtually without patrons in any quantity. Could we have a more felicitously placed table than this?"

The woman sighed and with great effort escorted them to a window-side table in a front corner, then threw their menus onto the table.

"Much better." Hortense beamed, but the woman, after telling them curtly that someone would be with them and mumbling something else in Italian, turned away. When they were all seated, Hortense leaned toward Immy and whispered, none too softly, "I guess the quality of wait staff that is available in Wymee Falls is not of the highest quality. Nor, it would seem, even mediocre."

The young man who waited on them—Antonio, his name tag said—was much nicer, maybe even high quality, thought Immy. He cheerfully got Drew a booster seat, some crayons, and a paper mat, and took their orders, serving them quickly.

Immy ordered Fettuccine Alfredo and split it with Drew, and Hortense was in heaven with a pile of lasagna that would have satisfied Garfield. The salads were adequate and the bread sticks nice and crispy, the way Immy liked them.

After announcing, "This yummy, Mommy," Drew went to work on the fettuccine with gusto.

A few customers arrived while they ate, but business was not booming. As the hour drew nearer to an actual mealtime, though, the tables started to fill up.

The three were poring over the dessert list when Immy spied a familiar figure coming from the back. Frankie! She was glad they weren't at the table next to the kitchen, or he would have seen them for sure. Could she remain *incognito* and tail him, report him to Ralph or Chief Emersen? How, when her mother and daughter were with her? But she had to alert the authorities.

Frankie hadn't twigged to them. He hurried through the room and pushed out the front door.

"Wait here," said Immy. "I'll be right back."

She dashed outside and caught sight of Frankie getting into his little sports car. His glass mufflers roared to life as he took off down the street. Immy flipped her cell phone open and dialed the Saltlick police department, afraid her call would go to a Wymee Falls station if she dialed 9-1-1.

Ralph answered. Immy smiled, glad it wasn't Tabitha.

"I just saw Frank Laramie. He's in Wymee Falls and he's in his own car. He drove north, away from his uncle's Tomato Garden restaurant. Turned right onto Holder Avenue."

"Good work, Immy," Ralph said, and Immy could tell he was grinning. He hung up, and Immy stayed outside for a while, waiting to hear the sirens and screeching brakes of cop cars chasing Frankie. She never heard them, but maybe he was being apprehended stealthily.

Immy re-entered the restaurant, and they ordered and polished off a shared serving of tiramisu. While she ate, Immy planned to check in at the Saltlick station on her way home. It wasn't until after Drew's bath and bedtime story, however, that she managed it.

The lobby of the station was dark, but lights were on behind the hallway door. Immy tried to open it, but it was locked. The area behind the glass, where Tabitha ruled during the day, was empty and dark.

Immy pounded on the hallway door until Ralph opened it an inch.

"Can I come back there?" she asked.

"No, you can't."

"No explanation, no apology, just, 'No, you can't?'"

"Immy, I'm glad you told us where to find Frank Laramie, but we're busy, and you have no business in the station right now."

Her scowl didn't affect him.

"But we're still on for tomorrow, right?" he said.

Maybe, she thought, that was his way of saying he'd spill the beans in private. She nodded and went home.

Twenty-Seven

Friday night came so quickly, Immy thought she must have missed a day. After she had started her job on Wednesday, the work had made both Thursday and Friday fly by. The job consisted mostly of filing and typing, but there were all sorts of different things to file and to type. She had eventually discovered that the puzzling items in her stacks at the corner of her desk, the recipes and newspaper clippings, were probably from her predecessor. Mike had no idea why any of them had been saved among the papers.

She had gone through the yellowing recipes and saved some that looked good. Most of the newspaper announcements were related to the Squires family. Immy didn't know any of them. They all seemed to live in and around Wymee Falls. She swept all of the clippings into a large manila envelope in case someone named Squires ever came by for them. Mike said his previous office helper had been a woman named Amy JoBeth Anderson, not Squires.

This anomaly piqued her detective curiosity a bit, but Mike wasn't interested in pursuing it, so Immy thought maybe she would try to track down Amy JoBeth some time on her own to test her skills. It would be fun to find out why all the announcements had been cut out, then left behind.

The minutes crept, with having to learn something new almost every hour, but the days evaporated. She left the office dead tired Friday.

She remembered the movie and dinner date with Ralph, though, so when she got home from picking up Drew on Friday, she changed into something a little nicer, a knit top instead of a tee.

"I think it's nice you're keeping company with that pleasant Ralph Sandoval," said Hortense. "He's so polite, even though I wouldn't wish a member of law enforcement as a mate for anyone, having suffered that fate myself."

Immy remembered the days when her mother wouldn't even talk about her father. It was a positive sign she did it so easily now, but it seemed that in her mind, Mother had Immy hitched to Ralph on their second date. She had no intention of marrying him. He was just a nice guy, and she thought it would be handy for her career to have an in with the local police. Her book had mentioned having handy contacts in local law enforcement. Wymee Falls was a lot bigger, and it might be better to date someone who worked there, but there sure was a lot happening here in the sticks lately, she had to admit. And Saltlick was more local.

She would try to keep in mind that she needed to get info from Ralph about Frankie. He and the chief must have been interrogating him when she had been at the station last night.

How exactly had they left it? She couldn't remember. Was Immy paying, or was Ralph? She had offered, but that was when she had assumed she would get paid Friday.

When her quitting time of two o'clock had rolled around, she had knocked lightly on Mike's door and entered when he called out.

"I guess it's time for me to go," she had said.

He glanced at the softly ticking clock on his desk. Once again, a candle smelling like walnuts burned beside it. "OK."

She stood, waiting for him to remember to pay her, but he returned his attention to the papers on his desk.

"It's Friday," she prompted.

"Hey, you're doin' great, kid. I think you'll work out fine. So I'll see you here next week?"

"Um, sure, and is it, um, payday today?"

"We didn't talk about that?" He screwed his little weasel face up in something that looked like pain. "Every two weeks works a lot better for me, kid. You only been here, what, three days? How about next Friday?"

"All right," she had agreed and taken herself home, remembering that Ralph had wanted to do dinner and a movie and she had offered to pay.

Immy always equated Ralph with the second-best Saltlick cruiser and was surprised to see him show up in a large, white pickup truck. He fit into it much more easily than the sedan.

"Where you wanna eat?" Ralph said. He shifted into drive and took them toward Wymee Falls, which held the only movie theater within fifty miles. "Let's eat first and then see the movie, OK? "

"OK." Immy fiddled with her purse strap. She had taken twenty dollars out of the bank. That was all she dared, since what was left was barely enough for groceries until next Friday. But twenty wouldn't be enough for dinner and a movie or even popcorn and a movie. Maybe she wouldn't eat anything, and she definitely wouldn't order popcorn.

"So, pick a place," he urged.

"Cracker Barrel?" Immy loved the cinnamon apples she had had there once when she was a little girl. She hoped they were still on the menu. If she just had those, maybe her twenty would stretch.

She would have to question Ralph at the meal since she couldn't do it during the movie.

When she ordered the apples Ralph asked if she wanted more to eat.

"Oh, I'm not very hungry," she said.

"I am. Should we get appetizers?"

"Ralph, I, um, I don't really have enough money to pay for all this tonight."

He grinned. "I wasn't going to let you pay, Immy. Go ahead and get something to eat."

As soon as Ralph dug into his meatloaf with mashed and gravy, Immy made her move.

"I guess you didn't have any trouble picking up Frank Laramie?"

Ralph looked up, a forkful of potatoes on the way to his mouth. "No, no trouble. Good job tipping us off. Appreciate it."

"And I guess you're holding him?"

"He's still in the cell tonight, yeah." The fork completed its journey and started another.

"So what part do you think he played?"

"Immy, I can't tell you any details."

"Not even if it's my uncle who was killed and Frank's uncle who may have done a hit on him? Not even if I'm a suspect?"

Ralph put his fork down and gripped his iced tea glass. "Especially if you're a suspect." He gulped half the glass.

"Keep your voice down. I don't want everyone in Wymee Falls to know. So I am still a suspect?"

"Chief isn't ruling anything out yet. We don't have a clear enough picture of—damn it, Immy, I'm not talking about this."

So she had no choice but to drop the subject of Frankie. She continued eating her still-delicious apples, savoring the cinnamon aroma and taste for a few minutes before she started in on Ralph about her next topic. "So what is Baxter getting charged with? I'm not a suspect on that case, anyway, right?"

"I guess you're not. Not sure what the charges are gonna be. Chief hasn't said what was in it, but he gave a report to the DA."

Immy ground her teeth slightly. "I hope he gets charged with something."

"Oh, at least the meth stuff. We got him on that, on purchasing the makings anyway, and that's enough."

"Good." Her fork squeaked as she scraped the bowl to get the last morsel of cinnamon apple.

"Sorry," Immy said, cringing at the sound.

The squeak didn't faze Ralph. "I thought you liked him."

Immy stared at Ralph. "Not after you told me he helped kill my father."

Ralph reddened. "I guess not."

"That was true, wasn't it? He really said that?"

"Yeah, you can ask Chief. Cross my heart." Ralph made an X on his chest with his beefy pointer finger. Immy gave him a sideways look. And people accused her of being immature.

"What about Huey's murder? I'm out of jail, so how can I still be a suspect?"

Ralph blushed yet again. "Your lawyer got you out, but I reckon you and your mama still are suspects since you get the diner and Hortense said she was going to kill him."

"Who told you she said that?"

Ralph's dark eyes widened. "Oh. Baxter Killroy told us that."

"Maybe you should discount it, then."

"We have to consider it."

Immy's fork clattered to the table. "Wait a minute. How could Baxter know what Mother said to Uncle Huey? Was he there?"

"Says he was. He says he was downstairs while they were arguing upstairs."

"But I was …" She almost said she was there, but they didn't know that, thanks to Mother. "Are you sure he was there?" She hadn't seen him.

Immy closed her eyes and tried to picture what she had seen. She had heard Hortense and Huey going at it as soon as she had opened the door. She had crept in, but where had she gone first?

She had peeked into the kitchen. It was possible Baxter had been hiding there, though the room had looked empty. A half-chopped head of cabbage was on the counter and she remembered thinking Clem was in the middle of making coleslaw.

Then Immy had remained in the empty dining room the rest of the time she was there. She had heard most of the shouting match, and her mother had not threatened to kill Huey, but she had left when Huey started counting off the seconds, telling Hortense she had to leave his office. When she heard Mother start for the stairs, Immy had left. Was it possible her mother had threatened him after that?

What she had always known was that it was possible her mother had killed him after she left, but she would never let herself believe that. No, Baxter was lying about Mother threatening Huey. He had to be.

"Immy," Ralph said. "I'm never sure of anything anyone tells us. A lot of people lie to the police." Did his look mean that he knew she had lied, if only by omission?

They saw a chick flick after the Cracker Barrel dinner. Immy supposed Ralph was trying for points by attending that kind of film, because he didn't seem to enjoy it much. She would have enjoyed a noir thriller, but this one was OK, too. The clothes and shoes weren't anything she would ever wear, probably couldn't even buy any of those things in Wymee Falls, but they were interesting to see. Immy wondered if people dressed like that in New York or maybe in Hollywood. She had been to Dallas and Fort Worth, and they sure didn't wear that stuff there. They dressed different than Saltlick folks but not like those movie stars.

When the movie was over, she told Ralph she had had a good time. On the ride home she racked her brains trying to think of ways to pump Ralph, but he wouldn't give out any more information about the murder investigation. Somehow, she couldn't see letting him unbutton her shirt to get him to talk. That had worked with that rat Baxter, but Ralph was a whole different animal. He hadn't even tried to touch her.

He walked her to the bottom porch step, said goodnight, and turned to leave. Immy realized she had enjoyed his company. It was nice being with someone who held doors and chairs and was concerned about how you were doing.

"Ralph?" Immy said to his back. "I had a really good time tonight."

He turned and stepped toward her.

"We could," she said, "we could do this again maybe."

Ralph's eyes were softening in the light from the single bulb on the porch. They were the color of dark chocolate. The cicadas were setting up a racket in the mesquite trees, and an early June bug popped against the screen door behind Immy.

"If you want to," she said.

Ralph smiled. His face lit up when he smiled. She had never noticed how nicely his lips curved, nor how soft they looked. Suddenly, they drew nearer. She stood on tiptoe. Ralph leaned down.

She got the shock of her life when they kissed. It was a long one. The initial jolt soon settled down to the level of a mild electric shock. Current ran through her from his lips and from the point where his hand touched the back of her neck.

After his soft, "Good night," and his departure, she waited for the noises in her ears to stop, for the fire in her body to burn down to a smoldering ember, for her sense of balance to return. After five minutes she realized it was going to take a good long while, so she mounted the stairs and went inside.

Hortense had let Drew stay up late, and Immy read her a Dr. Seuss book. Her mind strayed a bit from green eggs and ham as she felt the sparks from Ralph's contact continuing to course through her body. She tucked her daughter in and watched television with her mother for a while.

Drew was sound asleep when Immy went to check on her before getting herself ready for bed. She lingered at her daughter's bedside, breathing in her scent of bath bubbles and shampooed hair. She never wanted to be separated from her daughter again. Somehow, Immy had to figure out who had killed Huey, to preserve her way of life. If either Immy or Hortense were convicted of murder, Drew's little world would be shattered.

Twenty-Eight

Saturday morning, Immy awoke still feeling the impressions of Ralph's lips, his strong hands. In the shower she tried to cool her skin with vigorous rubbing. It still burned where he had touched her. She shook her head, reliving last night. Who would have guessed good old Ralph would have this effect on her?

Drew asked to go to the park after breakfast, so Immy volunteered to walk her there. Hortense wanted to get some of the season's last strawberries and make shortcake to go with them for supper. So Hortense left for the grocery store in Wymee Falls with a shopping list as they headed to the park, Drew skipping ahead in anticipation.

Summer was drawing near. The soft air whispered across the greening grass in Saltlick yards. Several neighbors knelt in the clay dirt, tending flowerbeds that were beginning to sprout weeds. Immy and Drew waved at those they passed and hollered, "Howdy."

Pink and blue wildflowers blossomed at the edge of the mowed lawn of the park. A family of at least three generations had eaten breakfast on one of the picnic tables, and now the adults sat, talking and sipping coffee while their children swarmed the sandbox, swings, and jungle gym. There were eight or ten children.

Immy pushed Drew on the swings, pondering when would be a good time to ask Mike Mallett for business cards. She wondered if she could get him to change her title from Assistant to Associate. Her name would look good underneath his on the door. The length of her name would make the sign look impressive.

"Hey, sugar." Baxter startled her out of her reverie. Damn, he was out of jail?

"Don't call me that. I'm not your sugar."

"Aw, sweetie, what'd I do?"

She whirled on him. "What did you do? Do you not know what you did?"

He backed off and dropped his smile. Was he afraid of her, little old Immy?

"You got my father killed! You stole money and gave it to me and made me a suspect! You …"

"Wait a sec, sugar. I did not steal that money I gave to you. I told you I found it."

"If you're telling the truth, you picked it up off the ground. It wasn't yours. You didn't try to find the owner, which was Huey's Hash and which I now own. It was stolen from me."

Baxter shrugged and started to walk away.

"Wait, there's more."

When Baxter turned back to her, she realized the picnicking family was staring at them. She lowered her voice but left the fire in her words.

"You lied to the police about my mother."

"Not exactly, sugar."

"Don't call me that." One of the men in the family started toward them. She lowered her voice again. "You told Ralph Mother threatened to kill Huey."

"She almost did. She said she wouldn't be sorry if he were dead. She said she wished he'd died in the robbery instead of her husband."

Drew's swing had come to a stop, but remarkably, she didn't ask for a push. Instead, she twisted her head around and watched the exchange, wide-eyed.

"How did you hear them? You weren't there."

"I wasn't? Who says?"

Immy squared her shoulders and lifted her chin for her lie. "I was there in back, in the alley, and your car wasn't there."

Baxter pondered this for a moment. "You were there? Did you go inside?"

She decided not to answer this. The man from the picnic table reached them, and Immy told him she was all right, just having a heated discussion. After he returned to his family, Baxter continued, still keeping his distance from her.

"Do the cops know you were there? They don't, do they?" How could she have thought that smile was sexy? It was mean. "But I could tell them, couldn't I?"

Damn. Immy had to think about that. Could he move her to the top of the suspect list again? Then she remembered what Ralph said about people lying to them. He wouldn't believe Baxter. She would bet the chief wouldn't either.

"Ha. With your word against mine, guess whose would win?" said Immy.

"I must have been in the storage room or outside helping unload supplies. I lied to the cops. I didn't hear anything that happened that day, but I did hear your mother say that exact thing another time. I overheard her and Hugh about a month ago, out back when he was leaving one night. She didn't think he was running the place right. She was afraid he was going to drive it out of business, and you and Drew wouldn't get anything from it."

That could have been true, Immy thought. Those were her mother's sentiments. She often lamented that Louie wasn't around to oversee his brother.

"But," Baxter continued, "I came back after he was dead, after your mother left. I told the cops I found him the next morning, but I saw him before then. Just didn't report it until morning. I figured maybe someone else would find him, but no one did until it was time for me to go to work."

"How long after he was dead were you there?"

He frowned. "How should I know? I don't know when he died. It wasn't long, though, from the looks of things. That sausage was frozen solid, and it was mush the next morning."

"Was anyone else there?"

"I didn't look around, sugar. I grabbed the money from the charity box on the counter, got in my truck and left. I ran outta there so fast I dinged Clem's pickup with my door, got that blue paint on my white pickup. Had a hell of a time scraping it off, too."

After Baxter sauntered away, acting like he'd won an argument, Immy absently gave Drew's swing a push.

"Sandbox, Mommy," Drew said, jumped off the swing, and ran to the sandbox, where three of the picnicking family's children were playing. Was Drew outgrowing the swings?

Immy followed behind while Drew ran across the park. OK, so Baxter wasn't there and didn't hear Mother threaten Hugh the day he died. But for some reason, Immy thought he'd told her the truth about returning a day before he told the police he did. Stealing the money from the charity box sounded just like something he'd do, the rattlesnake. Then he dinged Clem's truck and took off.

Wait a minute. He'd dinged Clem's truck? Clem had said he was out. She needed to talk to Clem. Soon.

When they reached home from the park, Hortense was in the kitchen, happily mixing shortcake batter. Every time she added an ingredient, it seemed to be necessary to taste a spoonful to make sure the balance was satisfactory.

They lunched on sandwiches while the shortcake baked, and then Drew felt like taking a nap. She didn't usually take one anymore, but the walk to the park and the climbing she had done on the jungle gym, after swings and sandbox, had tired her out.

Immy sat at the kitchen table, watching her mother test the cakes with toothpicks. She decided to make another list. She would list each person she deemed of interest along with the points for and against them.

First, Baxter. He was trying to blame Mother. Did that mean he was the killer? If he was a serious suspect, would he be out of jail now? He was a thief and probably had been planning to make meth, but killing? She wrote "maybe" next to his name.

Next, Xenia. She was still in the hospital, and Hugh's driver's license and credit card had been found in her possession. Did that mean she was the killer? If she had killed Hugh, wouldn't she have hidden those things better than that? Maybe she had been framed by the killer, or maybe she wasn't too bright. She wrote "maybe" next to her name.

Then, Frankie. He came from a violent family, full of hit men. Well, one for sure, but maybe more. He wasn't the type to do it himself. He would have his uncle do the dirty deed. So she wrote "no" by his name.

Guido, Frankie's uncle. There was no evidence for or against him except what Immy had overheard in the hospital parking garage, and the police didn't seem to be considering him very seriously. She wrote "maybe" next to his name.

She would have to put Clem's name down. His alibi didn't seem to hold up. If he'd gone out for cabbage, his truck wouldn't have been there. Was Baxter cleverly implicating him by slipping in the comment about Clem's blue truck being at the diner, or could Clem have returned from buying groceries by the time of the murder? Didn't they see each other? Could they be giving alibis to each other? She put "maybe" by his name, too.

She would not put her mother's name down, but she mentally put a "maybe" beside it. At the end of the list she added her own name but wrote "NO" after it.

This exercise wasn't getting her very far.

"Taste this, dear," said Hortense. She held out a spoon with a dollop of whipped cream on it. "Is it sweet enough?"

Immy licked the spoon. "Umm. Just right, Mother, as always. You know how to use your sugar."

Sugar. Drew had gone with Clem to leave messages spelled out in sugar packets. The messages were meant to draw suspicion away from Mother. How on earth had he thought that would work?

"Mother, when you were at Huey's Hash, and you had that argument with him before he was killed …"

"I did not threaten him bodily harm. At the interrogation, Chief Emersen tried to intimate I had done so. He tried to put the words in my mouth, actually."

"Did you notice anyone else there?"

"I have repeatedly told the police that the premises were vacant. Do you doubt my veracity?"

"No, no, I believe you, except for me being there, of course. Baxter even told me he lied about hearing you tell Huey you'd kill him. At least that day."

"If he was present, I did not detect the whereabouts of Baxter Killroy." Hortense shuddered when she said his name.

"I don't think he was there, Mother."

"If he was truly on the premises, he would have reported the conversation with more verisimilitude. For instance, it does not seem he mentioned that Hugh told me he had decided to effect the vending of his restaurant to the Giovannis and retain the proceeds for himself, which would leave you and Drew destitute. He laughed when he told me. If Baxter had heard and reported that, the police would know I had an excellent motive for wanting my brother-in-law dead."

Immy felt a quick shiver go through her. That gave her an excellent motive, too.

Twenty-Nine

Immy didn't need even a sweater tonight. Every day seemed warmer than the last lately. Soon enough, summer's sweltering heat would be here, but tonight, Saltlickians were out in droves, enjoying the warm evening as she strolled past on the way to Clem's. The diner had closed an hour ago, so he should be home by now.

She needed to find out why his truck was at the diner when Baxter was there, the day Hugh died, after the murder. She was hoping he would say he'd returned from buying groceries and had been in the food storage room or the locker, and that's why Baxter saw his truck out back.

The other reason she wanted to visit Clem was because he had never adequately heeded the warnings about Frankie's Uncle Guido. Any day now he might be a mob target. She thought maybe she should first stake out his house to make sure no hit men were lingering about. A quick perusal of her *Compleat Guidebook* made it clear she should provision herself adequately for a stakeout.

She was in luck as she approached the house with its cheerful, lit windows shining into his front yard. She spied an excellent place to carry out her surveillance, a clump of sage under his kitchen window. She had come prepared to watch all night, if need be. Her backpack held three peanut butter sandwiches and a package of animal crackers from Drew's lunch stash. She had also packed a thermos of iced tea but wouldn't drink that unless she was parched so she wouldn't have to pee. She couldn't figure out how people on stakeouts did that. At least, there was no mention in the *Guidebook* about how females

did it. There was a section that could only pertain to men. It said
to use the empty drink container. How could a woman do that?

In utter silence she crept to the window, parted the bush to
squeeze into the middle of it, and poked her head over the sill,
inch by excruciating inch. She first had to make sure Guido
hadn't already offed Clem or wasn't holding him hostage.

Clem sat at his kitchen table, his broad back to her. The huge
cat lay in front of him, getting stroked, its eyes narrowed in
pleasure. Three boxes of sugar substitute packets sat on the floor
next to them.

He was stealing from the restaurant! He had to be, otherwise
why did he have so much sugar and sugar substitute at his
house?

Fuming at his treachery made her hungry. She started to
unwrap one of her sandwiches, slowly, so it wouldn't make any
plastic crinkling noises from the wrapper. She needed to do
more observation. Moving her head to the edge of the window,
she could see his kitchen counter where a half-head of cabbage
sat next to a cutting board. That man sure did like cole slaw.
Cole slaw. Cabbage.

It was at that point that Immy put it all together. Clem
hadn't gone out for cabbage. There had been cabbage on the
counter in the kitchen when Immy peeked in the day Hugh was
killed. He might have been in the storage room, but he wasn't.
He had stolen those sugar packets, not for profit or to use, but to
make the murder look like a robbery. He had been there in the
diner, had heard Hugh tell Hortense he was selling Huey's
Hash. He may even have been upstairs. Immy envisioned Clem's
overburdened, probably enlarged heart breaking at that. Clem
had devoted his life to the restaurant, had never worked
anywhere else for twenty years. His passion for Hortense would
have extended, did extend, to Hortense's daughter and granddaughter, and now they would live in poverty.

Immy froze, going back over all the odd happenings. Had
Clem planted Huey's ID on Xenia while she was unconscious in

the hospital? Had he planted the money and checks on Baxter, knowing he would pick up a bag of abandoned money?

Had he killed Hugh?

The murder must have been his attempt to protect Hortense's family, an attempt gone horribly wrong.

Immy turned to leave, wanting to think this over at home. She was stopped by a very large man with a very large knife.

"So, do you have it all figured out now?"

"What? What, Clem? What would I have figured out?" Was her voice shaking? Probably. The rest of her body was.

"What exactly are you doing here?" He kept his voice low. No neighbors would be overhearing them. Before she could say she was trying to save his life, he rambled on. "You saw the box, didn't you? I hid them when you were here before. You figured out I took the merchandise to throw off the investigation. You know I only killed him to protect Hortense."

"Well, yes, Clem. I totally do not blame you for that."

She needed to figure out how to call 9-1-1 with the phone in her pocket. There was no way she could get out of this bush and around this huge man without getting sliced.

"But you know."

"Clem, I'll never tell anyone." *Until after I'm out of here.* She jammed the peanut butter sandwich she still held into her left front jeans pocket and fingered her cell phone in the other one. She had to flip it open to use it. Probably couldn't do that with it in her pocket. "I only came here tonight to make sure Frankie's Uncle Guido didn't bump you off."

"Why would he do that? Guido Giovanni?"

"Yes. I hear there's a contract out on you."

Clem's jovial smile creased his face for an instant with his belly laugh. "Guido? We're old friends, go way back. We went to high school together in El Paso."

The smile was gone as quickly as it had appeared. He waved the knife at her. "Come inside. Someone might see us out here."

The cat pussyfooted up to him and rubbed against his pant leg. "Good girl, Sheba," he said. "She saw you in the window. That's how I knew you were here." His voice sounded so conversational, like he was telling her he'd decided to add fried chicken to the menu.

He reached down to pet the cat, keeping the knife pointed at Immy. The blade caught the light from the window. It looked extremely long and extremely sharp.

Immy was pretty sure she shouldn't go inside his house, but how could she avoid it? He grabbed her arm, keeping the knife-holding hand out of her reach.

"Ow!"

Could she trip him? The man was solid as a brick wall, a slightly flabby but very solid brick wall. He yanked her and shoved her in the back door, into the kitchen.

"Know what?" said Immy, clutching at something to divert him. "I'm the owner of the restaurant now."

"Are you sure? Hortense doesn't own it?"

"No, no, the lawyer, Braden, he says I own it. It's in Huey's will."

"Huey." Clem spat into his kitchen sink. "He was going to sell the Double D."

Immy looked around the kitchen, hoping to see another knife somewhere, maybe a bigger one. She touched her cell again.

"I need to think about this," Clem said.

That was good. Thinking and not stabbing was good.

"Why is your hand in your pocket? You have a cell phone in there?" He snatched her hand out of the pocket and threw her cell phone across the room. The cover came off, and the battery went flying.

"Get in the pantry." He threw her in, and she sprawled on the floor as the door slammed shut.

He stomped away, and Immy got up from where she had fallen. It was a surprisingly big pantry with room for at least four normal people to stand. Maybe one and a half Clems would fit inside. It was dark, but her eyes adjusted after a few moments, and the light seeping under the door showed her shelves full of cans and jars and boxes on the three walls. Surely she would be able to bop him over the head with one of the giant tomato cans when he came in. OK, now, how to get him to come in?

"Clem," she called. "I have to go potty."

She heard his ponderous footsteps across the floor. He opened the door a crack.

Clem gave a little choke. "Does anyone know you're here?"

"Yes, yes. Everyone knows."

He stepped inside the room, closed the door, and switched the overhead light on.

"I'll bet no one does. You're playing detective again, and your mother doesn't like that. She's told me so. I don't think you told her you were coming here to spy on me." He coughed again, kind of a strangling choke.

"I did, I did tell her." Immy bobbed her head up and down. She took her sandwich out of her pocket, thinking there was something she should be remembering about Clem.

"See?" She thrust her sandwich toward him. "She made me these sandwiches."

Not true, but she could have.

Clem's throat gave a curious gurgle. "What … is … that?"

"A peanut butter sandwich."

Clem dropped the knife and turned, trying to get away from her. He grasped for the door knob and missed, slumped to the floor. "Allergic … peanuts …" He thudded to the ground, clutching his throat.

Oh, yeah. Clem was allergic to peanuts.

Immy kissed the sandwich and threw it down beside his massive, writhing body. She burst out of the pantry, picked up her cell phone and put it together. Called 9-1-1. And ran like hell.

Thirty

Chief Emmett Emersen and Immy sat on the green plaid couch, his shiny billed hat between them. Hortense tottered in from the kitchen, bearing a tray with a pitcher of iced tea and four glasses. Ralph Sandoval had carried in a chair from the kitchen, and Drew sat beside him on the floor, undressing the Barbie doll Ralph had brought for her.

Hortense banged the tray onto the coffee table, and after she lowered herself into the recliner, Immy poured drinks. She noticed Ralph used three sugar packets. The chief had given the four boxes from Clem's house to them after forensics finished with them. They now had a lifetime supply of sugar and sugar substitutes.

"Clem isn't talking," said Chief, "even with the swelling in his throat mostly gone. I know he confessed to you, Imogene, but that won't be enough to convict him." He turned to face Immy. "Do you think you could convince him to come clean?"

It was Sunday afternoon. Hortense, Immy and Drew had gone to church, and Immy's prayer of thanksgiving had been more heartfelt than ever before. They had just finished a chicken dinner when the Saltlick police had shown up.

"So you don't have enough evidence to put him away?" she asked. "I don't think I carry any weight with Clem. He wanted to kill me." Immy shifted on the couch with unease at Drew's rapt attention to the conversation.

"We don't have hard evidence," he said. "We do have his prints on the license and credit card he must have planted on Xenia Blossom, but a good lawyer can explain those away. There's no way to decipher his prints on the money and checks, they've been handled by too many people. But he probably left those for Killroy to find, then called us and told us Killroy had them. Of course, you had them by the time we looked for them on him. We're in the process of subpoenaing phone records and may be able to trace the anonymous calls to him."

"On what charge are you incarcerating Clem now?" asked Hortense.

"Assault on Imogene. Two neighbors saw him threaten your daughter with a knife. One of them called a while before you did, Immy."

"I guess I knew he was allergic to peanuts, but I didn't think of it right then. If I'd thrown my sandwich at him when we were outside, I could have gotten away sooner."

"He is violently allergic," said Hortense. "Merely being in the general vicinity of your peanut butter would have made him succumb very soon, whether or not you extended it in his direction." Hortense heaved a huge sigh. "I feel somewhat responsible. Clem's misplaced loyalty is what got him into such trouble."

"That and his crush on you, Mother," said Immy.

"Unca Clem in jail?" asked Drew.

"Yes, dear," said Hortense.

"Can we bisit him?"

"No."

"The reason I'm here," said the chief, "is to ask a favor of either you, Immy, or you, Hortense." He turned to Hortense. "Do you think you could persuade him to confess?"

"He'll do anything for you, Mother."

Hortense gave her daughter a doleful look, then capitulated. "I surmise I could undertake such an endeavor."

Emmett waited impatiently while Hortense stopped in the bathroom to fix her face, then they all walked out to the front yard.

Ralph and the chief had both come in the Shiny Cop Car. It rested on the valiant front yard grass, which was struggling to green up with the help of the usual frequent spring rains. The early iris Hortense had planted last year made a splashy display next to the trailer and swayed in the slight breeze.

"I'll walk back, Chief, if you want to drive Mrs. Duckworthy to the station," said Ralph. "It's a nice day."

"That's fine," said the chief, "but I need you there soon. Don't dawdle."

Ralph looked hurt that the chief would think he would dawdle. "I won't."

"Mommy, can we go to the pleece station with Geemaw?" asked Drew.

"Not today. Maybe another day."

"Is she arrested again?"

Ralph laughed. "No, she's not arrested. She'll be home real soon."

Drew ran back inside, probably to return to her Barbies, thought Immy.

Immy watched the chief hold the door for Hortense and drive off, thinking back to the day she had been driven to the station in the back seat. A puff of dust followed them down the road. Immy was sure Mother would be able to talk Clem into confessing. She could talk him into anything.

She realized Ralph was still standing beside her.

"Don't dawdle, Ralph," she said, looking up at him with a grin.

"I'm not dawdling, just need to ask you a question." He fiddled with his hair, and his face reddened.

"Well, ask it."

"What are you doing next Friday night?"

"I don't know. What are you doing?"

Meet Author Kaye George

Kaye George is a novelist and short story writer whose Agatha-nominated tale *Handbaskets, Drawers, and a Killer Cold* can be found in her collection. *A Patchwork of Stories* is available in either paperback or ebook formats.

Kaye does reviews for *Suspense Magazine* and also writes articles for newsletters and booklets.

She, her husband, and a cat named Agamemnon live together near Austin, Texas.

For more information visit www.KayeGeorge.com, or catch her at TravelsWithKay.blogspot.com, her solo blog. She joins other writers at AllThingsWriting.blogspot.com.

CPSIA information can be obtained at www.ICGtesting.com
234764LV00001B/13/P